Island
Christmas

Wildflower B&B Romance Series
Island Refuge
Island Dreams
Island Christmas

Island
Christmas

Wildflower B&B Romance 3

by
Kimberly Rose Johnson

ISLAND CHRISTMAS
Published by Mountain Brook Ink
White Salmon, WA U.S.A.

Scripture quotations are taken from the King James Version of the Bible. Public domain.

ISBN 9781943959051

The Team: Miralee Ferrell, Kathryn Davis, Nikki Wright, Hannah Ferrell, Laura Heritage
Cover Design: Indie Cover Design, Lynnette Bonner Designer

Mountain Brook Ink is an inspirational publisher offering books you can believe in.

Printed in the United States of America
First Edition 2015
1 2 3 4 5 6 7 8 9 10 11 12 13 14 15

ACKNOWLEDGMENTS

I'D LIKE TO GIVE A SPECIAL THANKS to everyone who had a hand in putting this book together. It would not be what it is without you.

And it is with gratitude that I thank each of you, my readers. If you enjoy *Island Christmas*, I hope you will tell a friend about it. I cannot do what I do without you.

Finally to my family and friends, thank you for your support and for believing in me.

CHAPTER ONE

RACHEL NARRELLI TUCKED ONE HAND INTO her jacket pocket and with the other, held tighter to her small son's hand as she gazed at the house that had changed the course of her life. Well, maybe the Wildflower Bed-and-Breakfast hadn't, but the people here had, and it felt wonderful to be back. She took in the old Victorian house that looked so much nicer than the first time she'd visited. The white paint on the exterior, now a little more than three years old, looked as good as the day they painted it. She snickered.

"What's so funny, Mommy?" Jason, her three-year-old son, tugged at her hand.

She squatted to his level. "I was thinking about the summer I spent here when you were in my tummy. I walked out that door," she pointed toward the covered porch, "when the man who was painting wasn't paying attention and painted *me* instead of the house."

Jason giggled, the childlike sound infectious. She pulled him into a bear hug. "We won't be here long, but I think you will like the B&B, Jasie. The owners are real nice. Mrs. Jackson is my new boss, too."

"What's a boss?"

She tapped his nose. "Someone who tells you what to do."

He grinned and placed a hand on each side of her face. "You're my boss, Mommy."

"That's right." She stood and took his hand. "Now be on your best behavior."

Little Jason, named after her late husband, or Jasie, as she so often called her active son, stood straight and raised his chin. She tried not to laugh, but he was so cute when he attempted to act like a big boy.

The screen door swung open and Zoe strode out, keys in hand, looking through her purse as she walked. She trotted down the stairs without looking up until her feet hit the pavement. "Rachel?"

She nodded. "It's good to see you, Zoe. I can't thank you enough for giving me a chance to cook with you."

"Don't thank me yet. You'll have to prove you are as good as your instructor said." She grinned and pulled Rachel into a hug. "I can't believe you are really here. I mean, I knew you were coming, but it's been so long." She seemed to notice Jason for the first time. "And who is this?"

"This is my son, Jason."

Zoe bent over and held out her hand. "It's nice to meet you, Jason. I'm Mrs. Jackson, but if it's okay with your mom, you may call me Zoe."

His eyes widened. "You're my mommy's boss."

Zoe chuckled. "That's right." She turned her attention back to Rachel. "Things have changed quite a bit since you left. A woman named Jill manages the B&B now. I think you'll like her. She actually reminds me a lot of you. Go ahead and get settled. I'll see you later at the restaurant."

"Okay." It was difficult imagining someone besides Nick running the B&B, but considering he was practicing medicine again it made sense to bring in a manager.

Zoe skittered off to her red convertible, the same one she

had when Rachel was here before. The car's top was up. Rachel thought it looked better down, but November weather was too cold and wet for that.

"Come on, Jasie. Let's go get settled. I hope we get the Poppy room, where I stayed the last time I was here."

Her son stayed glued to her until they stepped inside and she released his hand. Jill, the woman Zoe mentioned, sat at the reception desk. Her long dark hair cascaded to the middle of her back in soft waves. She looked to be in her early thirties and wore a pleasant smile.

"Welcome to Wildflower Bed-and-Breakfast. You must be Ms. Narrelli."

Rachel nodded. "Please call me Rachel. Ms. Narrelli makes me feel old." At twenty-six, she was *not* old.

Jill nodded then handed her a key and a card. "All the information you should need is on the card, but feel free to ask if you have a question. Mrs. Jackson requested you be assigned the Poppy room. I trust it will be to your liking."

Rachel nodded and wondered how this ultra-professional woman could possibly remind Zoe of her. A crashing sound in the sitting room accompanied by her son's shrieking cry sent her running into the room. She sensed Jill close behind. A lamp lay overturned on a room-sized rug that covered the wood floor, and a frowning man bent over to pick it up. When he stood his vivid blue eyes caught hers. "Is this little dude yours?"

Jason raced to her and clung to her leg.

Rachel rested her hand on his shoulder as his body trembled. "What happened?" Jason could be a handful at times. She bit her bottom lip, determined to remain calm and polite.

Jason looked up at her. "I was playing ring-around-the-rosie."

"Sorry about this," she said to Jill and to the man who stood nearby. "Jason, please apologize."

He looked to the ground. "Sorry."

"No harm done," Jill said, but her pinched smile indicated

3

otherwise.

The guy shrugged. "I'm sure I knocked over more than my fair share of things as a boy. Look, the lamp is fine." He placed it on the end table beside a leather chair.

Jason's head popped up, and he gazed with admiration at the man, who in turn winked at her son.

Jill turned to her. "I assume you know your way to your room?"

"Yes. Thank you."

"Excuse me then." Jill pivoted and left the room.

Jason held up his arms. "Up." Her precocious son, though very verbal for a three-year-old, still needed an afternoon nap, which he'd missed. She lifted him into her arms and warmed as he snuggled close.

The man stepped forward. "I'm Chris."

"It's nice to meet you. I'm Rachel."

He brushed a longish swoop of brown hair out of his eyes. "You've stayed at the Wildflower B&B before?"

She nodded as Jason went limp in her arms. Although he was a little guy, when he was completely relaxed, he quickly became heavy. "Excuse me. I should lay him down for a nap." She turned and trudged up the stairs, torn between wanting to visit with the attractive man and taking her son to the room.

As she settled Jason in his bed, she thought about Chris. He appeared to be in his mid-thirties. He kind of reminded her of Christian Bale except for the blue eyes and black-rimmed glasses. His dark hair that tickled his shirt collar only added to his appeal. Based on his trim physique she suspected he knew his way around a gym.

She smoothed the comforter over her sweet boy and went to the window. As she gazed out she wondered what Chris did for a living—not that it mattered. Since he was hanging out in the B&B's sitting room, he was probably here as a guest, which meant he was only visiting. Too bad. He intrigued her. Which was odd since he was the first man she'd noticed since her late husband's death. She pushed all thoughts of Chris aside. She had Jason to think about, and a man passing through their lives would do more harm than good.

CHRIS RAN A HAND over his five-o'clock shadow. The woman and her son were sure to liven things up. He'd been here a couple of days scouting for an investment property as well as a place for himself but hadn't found anything on his own. It was time to employ the services of a Realtor in the know. Tomorrow morning he had an appointment with a local agent to go over the inventory on the island. So far his search had turned up little.

He'd lived lean for the past five years to save up enough cash to buy an income maker. A duplex would be ideal, but the idea of running a B&B appealed too. Ultimately his dream was to live off the profits of his investments. Even though he loved his job as a software developer, he'd always been interested in investing in the local real estate, and ever since Wildflower Resort had come to the island, the value of property had grown exponentially. Too bad he hadn't had the money saved a few years ago.

He glanced toward the stairs where Rachel had been only seconds ago. The kid was cute, but his mom was even more so. Her husband was a lucky man. He wanted a family someday. He should have had one by now, but life didn't always turn out as expected—especially when his ambitions made slowing down long enough to meet the love of his life difficult.

He folded the paper he'd been reading before the rascal knocked over the lamp, and strode toward the stairs. He detoured to the dining room and grabbed a plateful of goodies. Fresh fruit, vegetable sticks, dip, and lemon bars graced the table. He filled a plate with fruit and veggies. This would have to tide him over until this evening. He had reservations at the much talked about resort restaurant, Wildflower Fresh. Though the name was simple, the place was famous for fresh Northwest cuisine.

Plate in hand, he went up the stairs to his bedroom at the end of the hall. The deep green accent colors and four-poster bed suited his taste—rich and masculine, but not overly fussy. He'd spoken with Nick, the owner of the B&B, about the décor, since the idea of owning a place like this intrigued him. The man told him that his wife insisted on redecorating almost all of the guestrooms after they were married. From what he'd seen in old pictures the place had originally been filled with Victorian antiques. As far as he was concerned, the change was for the better.

He devoured the snack and spent about an hour or so working on his current project. If he was going to make this island home, he wanted to be familiar with it before investing his life savings. He grabbed his winter jacket and slipped it on as he headed out to explore.

A path leading toward the Sound drew him, in spite of the cold. He hurried along not willing to waste a second. He stepped onto the pebbled beach and breathed in deeply. Peace settled over him. For the first time in his life he had no doubts. This was his future. He believed it to his core. He picked up a smooth pebble, flinging it into the Sound. It skipped twice.

"That the best you can do?"

He whirled around. The new woman at the B&B stood a few feet from him. "Rachel, right? Where's your son?"

She pointed off to the left where the boy stood near the water's edge staring at the Sound with slumped shoulders. "He wants to swim. I told him the water is too cold. He had to see for himself." She shrugged then bent down and picked up a smooth rock and flicked it at the water. It skipped four times.

He chuckled. "Competitive much?"

"Sorry." She shot him a sheepish grin.

He clasped his hands behind his back. "What brings you to Wildflower Island?"

She glanced toward her son, never fully allowing her attention to drift from him. "I've been hired as the new sous chef at Wildflower Fresh. I'm super excited to work with Zoe. She's the reason I went to culinary school."

"Really? So your husband followed you here to the island?"

She flicked an indiscernible look his direction. "My husband died a few years ago. It's just Jason and me now."

"I'm sorry." He understood her loss—had experienced more than his fair share. "I have reservations at Wildflower Fresh for this evening. The reviews have been impeccable."

"Let's hope they stay that way." She grinned and glanced at her watch. "I have to drop Jason at the sitter's house before I head to work. It's time to go, Jasie," she called to her son, and held out her hand. "I'll see you around, Chris."

He waved, then turned back to face the water. She was single and not a tourist. What were the chances two future island residents would be staying at the Wildflower B&B? He didn't believe in coincidence, and now, more than ever, wondered what the future on the island held for him.

CHAPTER TWO

TONIGHT WAS RACHEL'S FIRST NIGHT AT Wildflower Fresh and her nerves were shot. She rushed to gather Jason's bedtime stuff and enough toys and books to keep him occupied at the sitter's. She couldn't wait to get her own place so the sitter could come to her. Her hands shook as she stuffed his pajamas into his blue backpack.

Her cell phone chimed, and she snagged it off the dresser. "Hi, Tori."

Her sitter sneezed into the phone. "I'm so sorry for the last minute call, but I'm sick and can't watch your son."

Panic surged through her. She couldn't miss her first day of work! "Um okay. Maybe he could play in another room or something."

A hacking cough assaulted her ears.

"Never mind. I hope you feel better soon, Tori." She disconnected the call and plopped onto the bed.

Jason looked at her from his position on the floor where he'd been enjoying a picture book. "We go now, Mommy?"

"Not yet. Mommy needs to think." She didn't know anyone on the island other than Zoe and Nick. What was she going to do? Maybe Jill would know someone. "Come on, Jasie." She held out her hand.

He hopped up and tugged her toward the door. "I hungry."

"It's I*m* hungry, Jason."

"You hungry too, Mommy?"

She shook her head, giving up on correcting his grammar for now. They had to get their own place fast. Living at a B&B was fine for an adult, but she wanted privacy and access to a kitchen to fix healthy meals for her son. "I put celery sticks and peanut butter in your backpack along with crackers and a cheese stick." It wasn't much, but he ate like a bird unless he was having a growth spurt.

Jason pulled her toward the stairs. "I do it myself." He tugged his hand free from her grasp, then reached for the railing.

"I want you to hold my hand."

"No. I do it." He led with the same foot until he got to the middle then looked over his shoulder and grinned. "See." He turned back, and the next thing she knew he was tumbling. A scream ripped from his lips.

Or was that her own? Rachel raced after him.

"Whoa there." Chris caught Jason before he hit the landing.

Rachel slowed, breathing heavily. "You saved him! Thank you." She extended her arms toward Jason, who reached out to her from the safety of Chris's arms and drew Jason close. "You okay, honey?"

"That was funny." Her son giggled.

Leave it to a three-year-old to think falling halfway down the stairs was funny. He looked okay too—no blood or protruding bones. She inhaled deeply and let it out slowly, trying to slow her pulse.

"Never a dull moment with this guy." Chris winked. "I guess someone is pretty excited about going to his sitter's."

Rachel sighed, feeling much older than her twenty-six years. "I wish. My sitter is sick and cancelled a few minutes ago."

His brow furrowed. "What are you going to do?"

"I thought Jill might know someone. I can't miss my first day on the job."

"I'd offer to watch the little guy, but—"

"You have dinner reservations. Don't worry about it, Chris. Jason isn't used to being around men anyway." She took a step then paused. *Isn't used to being around men? Had she seriously said that?* Her cheeks flooded with heat. "That didn't come out the way I—"

He chuckled and raised a hand palm out. "It's fine. I understand."

"Have you seen Jill around?"

"Did I hear my name?" Jill pushed through the swinging doors that led to the kitchen and presumably her suite.

"Yes." Rachel moved toward her. "My sitter cancelled at the last minute and I start work at Wildflower Fresh in…" she glanced at her watch. "Thirty minutes. I was hoping you could recommend someone."

Jill's face lit. "As a matter fact, I can. My niece lives nearby. She's thirteen and is an excellent babysitter."

"I not a baby." Jason stuck out his bottom lip.

Jill chuckled. "Sorry there, little guy."

"I not little either."

"Quiet, Jason." Rachel touched a finger to his lips.

Jill breezed by her and stopped at the reception desk. "Alyssa watches children of our guests frequently, so I had business cards made up for her. She is great with kids, and I'd trust her with my own if I had any." She handed over a white card with blue and pink baby rattles on each side of the card.

"This is really short notice." Rachel couldn't imagine the girl would agree to a job with only a moment's notice.

"Don't worry. I happen to know for a fact she's free tonight. She's coming here to bake cookies with me, but I'm sure she'd much rather watch your son."

The knot in her stomach eased. "Okay. Thanks." She set Jason down. Maybe tonight wouldn't be a disaster after all. "How about you go sit at the table and eat a celery stick." She handed him his backpack.

"Okay." He skipped over to the table.

Satisfied her son would stay out of trouble for a moment she called the sitter. "Is this Alyssa?"

"Yes. Who's this?" the way-too-young sounding voice asked. Maybe this was a mistake. Surely Zoe would understand.

"Hello?"

"Sorry. I'm Rachel Narrelli. Your Aunt Jill gave me your card. I'm looking for a sitter."

"Oh!" Her voice took on an animated tone. "When do you need me?"

She looked toward the dining room table where Jason ate happily. "Right now. I'm staying at the B&B, and I'm in a huge hurry to get to work. My sitter is sick and cancelled at the last minute."

"I'll be right there."

"I can come get you."

She giggled. "I'm in the car with my dad. We were on our way over when you called."

Just then the front door opened, and a petite blonde girl and a man stepped inside. "Hi. I'm Alyssa, and this is my dad." She pocketed her cell phone.

The man held out his hand. "I'm Derrick."

Rachel quickly stuffed her cell phone into her purse. She took his hand and gave it a firm squeeze. "It's nice to meet both of you. Alyssa, my son, Jason, is at the table eating. He has plenty of food in his backpack. We're staying in the Poppy room. I'm really sorry to spring this on you. Are you sure you can handle him?"

"Of course. Plus Aunt Jill is here if I have any problems."

Rachel glanced at Jill who forced a smile. What was up with

the woman? One minute she was happy and helpful and the next she appeared to be put out. "Okay then. Jason, come here for a minute please."

Her son scooted off the chair and trotted to them.

"This is Alyssa. She will be watching you tonight."

He studied the girl for a moment then shrugged. "I like blocks."

"You do?" Alyssa asked with a lilt in her voice. "Blocks are my favorite. We could play after you finish eating."

"I done." He turned and headed for the stairs.

Alyssa giggled and followed him.

Derrick chuckled. "Don't worry about your son, Mrs....?"

"You may call me Rachel."

He grinned, perfect white teeth flashing at her. "Rachel. My daughter is beyond her years. Since her mom died she's taken over running our household. Were it not for my sister Jill stepping in and making sure Alyssa had a childhood, I think she would be a fifty-year-old in a teen's body." He looked to his sister. "Alyssa still needs to bake those cookies tonight. She's supposed to bring three dozen chocolate chip for the bake sale at school tomorrow."

"Don't worry. I'll make sure they get baked, and I'll bring her home when she's finished." Jill grinned. "I'm looking forward to tonight with my favorite niece."

"She's your only niece. You don't want anyone to think you play favorites." Derrick planted a kiss on Jill's cheek. "You're the best, sis." He nodded toward Rachel.

"I agree you are the best, Jill. Thanks for saving me tonight." Rachel followed after Derrick. "I'll walk out with you. I'm on my way to work." Why had she said that? It must be her nerves, and losing her sitter at the last minute didn't help with her nerves. She had to calm down, or she was liable to cut off a digit tonight.

She strolled beside him. "I'm sorry about your wife. How long ago did she die?"

He glanced in her direction. "Thanks. She was in a car accident two years ago." His Adam's apple bobbed. "It's been rough."

"I understand."

"Thanks, but unless you've been there, there is no way you could."

She paused and looked him in the eye. "My husband died of a cancerous brain tumor two weeks after we were married. We had no idea he had something wrong with him until it was too late." She shook her head. "But you're right. I shouldn't claim to understand the kind of love you and your wife shared." She left without looking back, but the surprised look in his eyes made her wish she'd stayed silent. He had no way of knowing she had never loved her husband.

She slid into her navy Subaru Forester. Time was not on her side today. She should have come to the island yesterday. Should have, could have, but instead she chose to spend one more day at her parents'.

CHRIS WALKED INTO WILDFLOWER Fresh and strolled toward the hostess. "I have a reservation for one. Chris Campbell." As the hostess checked off his name and gathered a menu, he looked around. The place felt warm and inviting. The rich tones of the cherry wood paneling appealed to him. A large stone fireplace along the far wall gave a cozy and inviting feel. The light clinking of silverware on dishes interplayed with a low rumble of voices and dinner music.

"If you will follow me, Mr. Campbell, I will show you to your seat." The hostess wove her way to the far side of the room and seated him along a bank of windows that faced a small lake with white lights strung through the trees, outlining the lake. "How is this?"

He could hear noise from the nearby kitchen, but the view made up for it. "It's fine. Thank you." He sat with his back to the kitchen so he had a good view of the entire restaurant. With the holidays fast approaching, he wondered how busy this place would get. It wasn't exactly a destination vacation spot, but at the same time, who wouldn't want to be pampered in such an idyllic setting?

A dark haired woman wearing a black pantsuit strode in his direction. She smiled. "Good evening, sir."

He nodded as she walked past and on into the kitchen. He'd noticed her picture on a wall as he made his way into the restaurant. If memory served she was the owner—Piper Grayson. She must be a hands-on kind of boss. He wondered how Rachel would deal with that considering how stressed she appeared earlier this evening. But then maybe she was frazzled because of her sitter situation. Either way, he hoped she didn't mind having the owner hovering over her.

A crash in the kitchen made him jump. That couldn't be good. He peered over his shoulder as Rachel rushed into the dining room, her face pale. She hesitated. He stood and blocked her path. "You look like you might appreciate a friendly face. Join me?" He drew her to the seat opposite his.

She shook her head but sat down. "I'm sure I'm not allowed."

"Relax. If your boss says something, I'll tell her I demanded to know what all the commotion was about."

Her eyes widened. "Are you? Demanding?"

"Requesting nicely. What happened? Are you okay?"

She sighed and opened her mouth to reply, but before she could speak his waiter approached, curiosity lighting his young eyes.

"Are you ready to order?"

"Yes. I'd like the prime rib with baked potato and a dinner salad with ranch dressing. I'll have water to drink."

The waiter turned to Rachel, brow raised.

"Nothing for me. Thanks."

Chris handed the young man his menu, then focused his attention on the wounded woman across from him. "Are you on break?"

"Zoe told me to take the rest of the night off."

"Ouch. What did you do?"

Her eyes watered. "You don't want to know. The worst part is, Mrs. Grayson, the owner, walked in, and I was trying to show off and impress her. The only thing I managed to do was make myself and Zoe look bad." She buried her face in her hands.

His heart melted for Rachel. She clearly didn't need one more thing to go wrong tonight. "Have you eaten?"

"Technically no, but we sample enough food to make sure it's seasoned correctly that I feel as though I have." She moved to stand.

"Please stay. I know it's selfish of me, but I'd like the company."

She looked around. "Maybe I could visit for a few minutes."

"Good. I know your stay on the island got off to a bad start, but I'm sure it will only improve from here."

She chuckled. "I hope so. If every day turned out like this one…" She shook her head.

He grinned. "You mentioned coming to the island once before. If you don't mind me asking, what brought you here?"

She sat back and a sparkle lit her eyes. "I can laugh about it now, but at the time that was a pretty difficult time in my life. When my husband was on his deathbed he asked me to go to his parents' house and find a ring he'd stolen and hidden as a child, and return it to his grandmother. The problem was, he couldn't remember where he'd hidden it. My in-laws were devastated with the loss of their son and sold the B&B to Nick."

"Wait a minute. You mean to tell me your husband's family owned Wildflower B&B?"

She nodded. "Small world. Right?"

"For sure." He leaned in. "Tell me more."

"I secured a place at the B&B for the summer hoping to figure out a few things while I looked for the ring."

"Nick and Zoe didn't mind you snooping around?"

She chuckled. "That's another story, but let's say in the end they helped and Nick's nephew ended up finding it." Rachel's face appeared more relaxed than it had since he'd met her.

"I'd love to hear the rest of the story sometime."

"Maybe you will." She glanced over her shoulder. "I should go."

"Please stay."

Tension immediately filled her face. "I'd better not. If Mrs. Grayson comes out here and sees me like this, I may not have a job to come back to tomorrow. I trust Zoe will smooth over what happened in the kitchen, but I don't want to push my luck. Right now I'm going to visit the gift shop. I promised Jason a postcard of the place where I work."

Disappointment shot through him. "Understood. Maybe I'll see you tomorrow. Will you still be staying at the B&B?"

"Our reservation is through the end of the week. I hope to find a place for myself and Jason by then." She stood and pushed in the chair. "The prime rib was a good choice. To use a much overused word, it's a-ma-zing."

"Good." He didn't want her to leave yet. It was nice having someone to talk with. "May I walk you to your car?"

"No, thanks. I'm detouring to the shop."

Right. She'd already told him that. Too bad he couldn't come up with a good reason to visit the gift shop right now. She seemed like she could use a friend.

"Your order will be ready in a few minutes. See you, Chris." She hustled through the dining room and out of his sight.

He shook his head. He'd met Zoe and had no doubt Rachel's words were correct. Zoe would indeed smooth things over with Piper, but it was too bad she needed to. Poor Rachel. Trouble seemed to follow her.

He gazed onto the lake and noted the dock. A Christmas

tree at the end lit in a riot of colors grabbed his attention. Why hadn't he noticed that sooner? It seemed odd to have a Christmas tree on a dock, much less have one up before Thanksgiving, but he knew some people couldn't wait.

Piper entered the dining room, wearing a serious expression.

"Excuse me," he said.

She plastered on a smile. "Yes, sir?"

"I was curious about the tree on the dock. Why is it *there* for starters and up so soon?"

She peered out the window, and her face softened. "My husband must have put that up today. I know it's early, but there's a lot of decorating to do, so some things like that tree are up prematurely. We go all out for Christmas, including decorating the dock. It may seem odd to some people, but we enjoy it being there."

"I look forward to seeing the decorations. Did he string all those lights too?"

"His landscaping company did. Those stay up year round." She returned her focus to him. "I'm Piper Grayson, the owner of the resort. Are you a guest at the resort?"

"No. I'm staying at the Wildflower B&B."

Her smile widened. "That's a wonderful place. It was where I first stayed when I arrived on the island. I hope you enjoy your visit, Mister…"

"Campbell. But please call me Chris." He pulled his business card from his pocket out of habit and handed it to her. "I specialize in software and web design."

"Okay. Thanks." She slid his card into her pocket. "Enjoy your meal, Chris."

He almost groaned but caught himself. He was here to relax, not drum up more business. He was busy enough. Like they say, old habits die hard.

The hostess rushed to Piper and spoke softly. He couldn't hear her words but whatever she'd said caused Piper to hustle toward the exit.

His meal arrived and he wasn't disappointed. Never one to linger over food, he wolfed it down in a matter of minutes. The only thing missing was someone to share the experience with. Rachel was right. It was a-ma-zing. He grinned at her exaggerated enunciation of the word. He finished off his water, paid and left a tip, then stood to leave.

A commotion at the door grabbed his attention. Curiosity drew him. Flashing lights in the parking lot shot alarm bells through his head. What had happened? He peered through the glass doors and spotted medics hovering over someone. The person next to him said a woman who worked here was unconscious.

CHAPTER THREE

RACHEL'S HEAD POUNDED. WHAT WERE ALL these people doing around her, and why was she on the ground? A shiver ran through her. "Excuse me!" She felt like she was shouting, but her voice sounded barely above a whisper. She grabbed at an arm that seemed to float overhead.

"She's conscious." A blurry-faced man held two fingers over her face—or at least she thought it was two. If only she could focus. She blinked rapidly trying to clear her vision. "How many fingers am I holding up?"

"Two?"

"What's your name?"

"Rachel. What's all this about, and why am I lying down and who are you?" She knew that voice. "Nick?" She tilted her head to the side as his face came into focus. "It *is* you. What are you doing?"

"Piper called and told me you'd passed out in the parking lot. I told her to call 911 but decided I should swing by and see if I could help."

She tried to sit up, but Nick quickly held her shoulder in place so she couldn't.

"Take it easy, Rachel. I don't want you to move yet. Do you hurt anywhere other than your head?"

She shook her head and winced—bad idea. "Nick, I don't know what happened. I was heading to my car and the next thing I know..."

"How did you feel before you passed out?"

"I passed out?"

"It appears so. No one actually saw you, so we aren't sure how long you were unconscious."

"Oh boy. That sounds bad."

"Can you describe how you were feeling this evening?"

"Stressed, anxious... I went to the gift shop and looked around for quite a while then began to feel light headed and figured I should go back to the Bed-and-Breakfast. It's been a rough day and an even rougher evening."

"Do you have any underlying conditions I should know about?"

"No. At least none that I know of." Panic surged through her. What if there was something seriously wrong with her? Her son's dad had died of a brain tumor—if she died Jason would be all alone. Well, there were her parents, but still...

"Okay, then. I think it's best you go to the hospital and have some tests run. I suspect you had a vasovagal attack, but I'd like to rule out a few other things. Were you injured when you fell?"

"What is a vasovagal attack?"

"It's nothing serious and very common in young people. It basically means you fainted due to a rapid heart rate drop. I'm more concerned about any injury you may have sustained in falling."

Rachel squeezed her eyes shut. This couldn't be happening. Her head hurt as well as her back, but neither was excruciating. She described her pain to Nick, then allowed the paramedics to load her into the ambulance. As they lifted her onto the gurney, she had a view of the parking lot. At least there wasn't a huge crowd gathered around watching. She spotted Chris and sighed. She could add embarrassment to her growing list of things that had gone wrong today.

The rest of the evening flew by in a blur of doctors and tests. By midnight she was exhausted, and all she wanted was to snuggle beside her baby boy and sleep. Instead she lay on a hospital bed in the emergency department of a tiny hospital that had not been on the island the last time she had been there. Things had changed more than she'd realized.

A nurse glided into the room wearing a smile. "Ms. Narrelli, the doctor signed the paperwork, and you are free to go."

Finally. Joy washed through her. "Thank you. Is there a cab service I can call to take me to my car?"

"There's a gentleman in the waiting room. He said he would be delivering you home."

Relief washed over her, and she quickly prepared to leave. That was nice of Nick to stick around and save her the expense of a cab. Once again he was coming to her rescue.

"These are your after-care instructions along with your diagnosis." The nurse handed her a few papers. "Would you like a wheel chair or are you up to walking?"

"I'm fine. Thanks." Although slightly surprised the nurse hadn't insisted on a wheelchair. She remembered seeing people walk out of the ER back home too, so they must not require it unless admitted.

She glanced at the diagnosis. *Vasovagal attack.* Which she already knew since the doctor had explained her diagnosis and all that entailed. This must be in case she forgot what he said. She walked into the emergency department's waiting room and looked for Nick.

"Hey there."

She spun around to the left. "Chris. Are you the person waiting to take me to my car?"

"Actually, I was instructed that you are not to drive until tomorrow. I'll give you a lift to your vehicle in the morning.

Right now, we both need to get back to the B&B. You're a popular lady. Piper stopped by to check on you, but no one would tell her anything or allow her to see you, so she left."

"No kidding. That was really nice of her."

"Yeah. So why the frown?"

"Just thinking. Tonight is going to cost me a small fortune in insurance deductibles and babysitting. If I'd been thinking clearly I wouldn't have agreed to the ambulance ride to the hospital." She shivered. At this rate she'd never be able to afford a little place for herself and her son. She hoped there was a good selection of rentals because after tonight, she wouldn't be able to put a down payment on a house any time soon.

This island held a special place in her heart, and her dream since leaving it three years ago was to move back and make a life for herself and Jason. Would that dream ever become a reality?

CHRIS LOOKED RACHEL OVER from head to toe. He felt bad for her and was glad he'd thought to come check on her before heading to the B&B for the night. The longer he'd waited the more concerned he'd become, but other than her drooping eyelids that threatened to cover her deep brown eyes and her somewhat slumped shoulders, she appeared to be doing great. Anyone would be worn out after the ordeal she'd had this evening. He hadn't been the one to pass out and spend several hours in the hospital, and he was more than ready for his comfy bed.

She slid the band off her ponytail and massaged her head. Her raven colored hair cascaded to her shoulders and looked silky soft. Yep, she looked good. "Thanks for coming for me." Rachel shot him a look filled with gratitude.

"I'm happy to help."

She swayed slightly.

He shot his arms out to steady her. "You sure you're okay?"

"Just crazy tired. Aside from the day I gave birth to Jason, I think this has been the longest day of my life."

"Yeah, I get that." He kept a hand on her elbow and gently guided her outside to the parking lot. After making sure she was seated, he closed the door and rushed around to the driver's side of his black Prius. The sooner he delivered her to the B&B the better. She was ready to drop.

Comfortable silence filled the car as he whisked them to the bed-and-breakfast. He pulled into the driveway and parked in the same spot he'd vacated earlier in the evening. "I have an appointment with a Realtor in the morning. Do you think you could be ready to go by nine?"

"I'm not sure. How about we play it by ear. If I can't catch a ride with you, I'll figure something else out."

"Okay." He slid out and moved around to get her door, but she was already out and heading up the stairs.

She stopped, her hand resting on the railing. "Thanks for tonight. We've just met, yet you were there for me." She shook her head. "You're rare, Chris." She opened the door. A dim light illuminated the stairwell and together they plodded up the stairs. At her room she rested her hand on the doorknob. "Goodnight."

"Sleep well, Rachel." His heart did a little pitter-patter at the look in her eyes. He knew that look. Had felt it himself a few times in his life. Wanted to feel it again, but now was not the time.

"You too." She slipped into her room and closed the door softly.

He moved to the next door and went inside. He couldn't shake the feeling that his life had been permanently altered tonight. But at thirty-five he was too old for Rachel, he didn't want the complication of a relationship right now, and then there was his family medical history. Rachel did not need to be subjected to that. She'd already lost one husband—not that he was thinking marriage, he barely knew her. But he had to think about those kinds of things when he was attracted to a woman. Rachel would remain in the friend zone. It was best that way for both of them.

CHAPTER FOUR

CHRIS SAT AT THE BREAKFAST TABLE across from a family of four. Rachel and her young son had yet to show. He forked a bite of the most wonderful pancakes he'd ever eaten into his mouth. A commotion in the other room drew his attention.

"I hungry, Mommy. Hurry!"

He grinned. That was definitely little Jason.

The boy dragged his mother into the dining room. A scowl covered his face.

"Good morning, Jason. Rachel." Chris's eyes met Rachel's as she lifted her son onto the chair at the end of the table.

"Good morning." She offered a weak smile that didn't reach her eyes.

"How are you feeling?" She looked like she could have used a few more hours of sleep based on the dark circles under her eyes.

"I'm fine. Thanks again for waiting for me last night."

"You're welcome. Hey, Jason, you've got to try the pancakes, they are the best ever."

The boy's eyes lit, and his head whipped toward his mother. "I love pancakes," he said in a stage whisper.

"That's right." She took the plate Chris passed to her and forked a single pancake onto her son's plate, then poured syrup over the top and cut it into bite-sized pieces.

"He doesn't like butter?"

She shook her head. "Neither of us use butter on our pancakes."

He sipped his coffee and took delight in watching Jason devour the pancake his mother had cut up. The family across from them excused themselves, leaving him alone with Rachel and her son. "When do you think you will be ready to go, so I can drop you off at your car?"

"As soon as we finish eating. In fact, I have an appointment as well this morning, so we should get a move on. I don't want to be late. Jason and I are looking for a rental home." She bit her bottom lip. "Oh no."

"What's wrong?"

"Jason's car seat is in my car. He can't ride in yours without one."

Jill swept into the room. "I didn't mean to eavesdrop, but I heard your dilemma, Rachel, and I don't mind keeping an eye on Jason while you run over and pick up your car."

"Are you sure?"

"I am. My niece had a great time with him until she had to go to sleep since she has school today. Her dad came by early this morning and took her home to get ready for school."

"I'm so sorry about last night."

Jill waved a hand. "Things happen. Don't worry about it. Jason was a good boy, and after I read him a few stories he went right to sleep."

"I'm glad. Thanks again for rescuing me." She chuckled dryly. "Although I think it may have been better if I'd called in sick."

Chris pushed back from the table and stood, catching Rachel's eye as he did. "Can you be ready in ten minutes?"

"I'll be ready and waiting." She downed a glass of orange

juice then propelled her son up the stairs.

Chris followed a little more slowly. He felt bad for Rachel and wanted to be there for her, as a friend. He didn't have a lot of friends and looked forward to forming some good relationships in his new life here on the island.

He had been a workaholic, but he was well on his way to following doctor's orders and taking life at a less stressful pace, leaving room for fun and relaxation. He'd cut back the number of clients he took and was being more selective. Some people were more stress than the job was worth. According to his doctor, his future depended on his ability to reduce the stressors causing him tension.

His dad had died at forty-two from a heart attack, and his grandpa had died even younger. He didn't want to follow in their footsteps. No, he planned to live many more years. Diet and exercise, or lack thereof, played a role in each of their deaths, but even though his job required he be at a computer for much of the day, he'd always been careful to eat properly most of the time and get plenty of exercise.

He quickly brushed his teeth and tidied his room. He didn't want Jill, or whoever it was that cleaned the bathroom and made his bed every day, to think he was a slob. He pocketed his wallet and stepped into the hall. He met up with Rachel and Jason at the stairs. "Fancy meeting the two of you here." He grinned.

Jason held out his hand to Chris. "I want you. Not mommy."

Rachel's mouth opened slightly and shock registered in her eyes, but she recovered fast. "If Chris doesn't mind."

"Not at all." He grasped the boy's hand and together they went down the stairs. Chris's heart turned to mush, like it had done when his parents gave him a puppy at the age of ten. He'd loved that dog until the day she died. Ruby was a beagle and easy to love, much like this little boy who'd slipped his warm hand inside Chris's.

Jill stood at the bottom with a box full of toys and books. "We keep this stuff around for young families. I thought you might enjoy playing in the sitting room, Jason."

He nodded, tugged his hand from Chris's. "'Bye, Mom and Chris." He skipped into the sitting room.

"Well, I can see when I'm not wanted." She grinned at Jill. "I won't be too long. Thanks again."

Chris opened the door for her then closed it behind them. "So you're looking for a rental on the island?"

"I am. I'd hoped to buy, but after last night, I think renting would be a better idea for now."

He nodded, not sure if she was talking about her job or the expense last night's trip to the hospital had surely cost her. Maybe she meant both. He opened the car door, and after she was settled, he hustled to his side. "Where were you living before you came here?"

"With my parents. After I had Jason, I attended culinary school and earned my associates degree in culinary arts. I worked in a little café near my parents for almost a year and then landed the job here."

Her story somewhat surprised him. She hadn't mentioned her husband at all. He'd assumed the man had died after Jason was born, but it sounded like she was pregnant when he'd passed away.

His heart hurt for this surprisingly resilient woman. It must be difficult to have experienced that kind of loss at such a young age. He knew what it felt like to lose loved ones. It's what drove him to be successful at a young age and what drove him now at thirty-five to find a quieter and slower-paced lifestyle. He pulled into the resort's parking lot. "Where's your car?"

"Around back in the employee parking."

He frowned. If that were the case why had she come out through the main entrance last night? Maybe she'd been more disoriented than he'd realized. He followed a sign directing the way to employee parking and stopped beside her vehicle.

"I never imagined a place like this would exist on Wildflower Island when I first came here a few years ago, but I'm so glad it does. I had hoped for a tour of the place last night, but I didn't get to work early enough and well, you know how my evening ended." Rachel released her seatbelt and opened her door.

Compassion filled him. "Maybe we could tour it together sometime. If you have a few minutes we could do a quick walk through right now. I have the time." He wasn't much into architecture or that kind of thing, but he rather liked the masculine appearance of this resort. The outside resembled a mountain lodge with its stonework and use of natural wood, and he wouldn't mind exploring the inside. He'd gone straight to the restaurant last night without giving his surroundings much thought.

"That would be fun, but I promised Jill I'd be quick. Rain check?"

"Sure." He pushed down disappointment but determined to find a way to spend more time with Rachel.

"Thanks for the ride." She gave a little wave then pulled open the door to her Subaru.

He watched her drive away and decided to take a walk and explore the resort before going to his appointment, since he had time to spare. He drove around to the front of the building, parked, then ambled toward the lake. He passed a large fountain feature near the entrance and continued onto a pathway of pavers that meandered toward a pristine lake. Few people were out and about, but he noted a couple of joggers on the far side of the lake. Why people chose to jog in cold weather he'd never understand, then again, he preferred to work out in a gym. The treadmill was more his style. He hadn't found a gym on the island, so he probably should invest in a treadmill.

The Christmas tree on the dock that he'd noticed last night was still lit, shining vibrant colors. He had a thing about Christmas decorations being up before Thanksgiving, but in this case he'd excuse the faux pas. Piper's explanation about there being too many decorations to put up in a short time made sense.

A worker with a box filled with Christmas lights stopped beside a planter. "Good morning."

Chris nodded to the man who matched his own six-foot height. He wore a Seahawks stocking cap and a flannel jacket. "Does the resort do anything special for Christmas?" He figured they must since they'd "decked the halls" so well.

The man pulled out a string of lights. "My wife is a huge fan of Christmas, so the entire month of December will have special activities."

"Oh, you're Piper's husband? I'm Chris Campbell, a new resident of Wildflower."

"Welcome to the island. I'm Chase Grayson. This place has grown quite a bit since the resort opened. I hope that doesn't bother you. Then again why would it? You're new."

Unsure if being new was a bad thing or not, he decided to think the best of the man. "I came here for the slower pace. I'm looking for peace and quiet. The fact that this island, aside from the resort, feels like stepping back in time is exactly what the doctor ordered. Is there a schedule of events for the holiday, and is it open to the public?"

"Yes and yes. The schedule is online or you can get a copy at the concierge desk. All events are open to the public. Do you have kids? We do a fun sleigh ride that a lot of families enjoy."

Chris chuckled. "No, but how does that work without snow?"

"There are wheels on the sleigh. We haven't had snow in a number of years, but it's been known to happen." Chase shrugged. "I suppose you have to use your imagination a little, but it's a lot of fun. The kids love it."

Chris thought of little Jason and imagined he'd get a kick out of a sleigh ride, snow or not. He glanced at his watch. "I'll be sure and check it out. Thanks. Maybe I'll see you around."

He strolled to his Prius. He'd be right on time to the Realtor's office.

RACHEL HAD GONE BACK to the B&B for Jason as soon as she'd retrieved her vehicle. It would have been nice to do this without him, but she couldn't expect Jill to watch him all day. Now she sat facing Debbie Faucet, her Realtor. "I'm looking for something small. A single level with two bedrooms and a decent fenced yard."

Debbie clicked through listings on her computer and paused. "There are two houses that meet your specifications. Do you want to take a look now?"

Only two? Somehow she'd expected a better selection, but this was Wildflower Island and she should have known better. Rachel let out the breath she hadn't realized she'd been holding. "Yes! That would be great. I want to get out of the B&B as soon as possible and settled before the holidays."

The front door of the office opened, and Chris strode in. His cheeks looked a little windblown with their red tone. She'd noticed he hadn't left the resort when she did. He must have gone exploring. She couldn't blame him, even if the temperature was only in the fifties with a strong breeze.

He nodded. She offered him a smile. She liked the man and especially appreciated that he hadn't made her feel awkward about her medical issue the evening before. Debbie's husband, the other Realtor in the office, greeted Chris.

Debbie stood. "Would you like to follow me?"

Rachel gathered her jacket and purse. "That would be best. Come on Jason." She held out her hand to her son who played at a child-sized table in the corner.

"Ah," he groaned. "Do we have to go, Mommy?"

"Yes."

He tucked his chin to his chest, and his shoulders slumped as he shuffled his feet and eventually made his way to her side. She scooped him into her arms. At the rate he was moving, she'd have to leave for work before they even made it to the car.

Chris chuckled. "Hey there, buddy. Don't you want to go pick out your new house?"

Jason's face lit at the sound of Chris's voice. He clearly hadn't noticed the man until that moment. "I like the B&B. It's fun."

"Having your own bedroom will be fun too," Chris said.

Jason buried his face into her shoulder. She mouthed thanks to him and followed after Debbie.

"If you lose me, you have my number?" Debbie held the door for them.

"Yes, but I won't lose you." She was exceptional at driving. Call it a hobby or whatever, but when Jason was a fussy newborn, she'd put him in the car and they'd drive for hours. She'd become a very good driver in all types of road conditions and especially enjoyed winding roads. Her parents thought she was nuts, but those hours behind the wheel gave her clarity about her future and the direction she should go with her life.

Ten minutes later, they pulled into the driveway of a single-story white cottage. It looked uncomfortably small from the outside, but she was willing to give it a look.

"I hate it!" Jason wailed. "I want to go to the B&B. I like it there."

Confused at why her son had such strong emotions about a place he'd only stayed at for a day, Rachel tilted her head to face him. "Come on, buddy. We need to at least look."

Jason crossed his arms and stuck out his lower lip. With a sigh, she got out of the car, opened his door, unclasped his car seat restraints, and hoisted him into her arms. He tried to wiggle free, but she held strong. It was times like this she wished for a dad for her son, but what man wanted a ready-made family? None that she'd met.

Her thoughts drifted to Chris. Jason adored him. She had to admit, the man was a jewel among men, but he had to be close to ten years her senior. That wouldn't stop him from being someone her son could look up to. Jason needed good male influences in his life. But she had a feeling they wouldn't be seeing much of Chris once they moved out of the B&B.

CHAPTER FIVE

LONG PAST WHEN SHE SHOULD HAVE been in bed sleeping, Rachel sank onto the couch in the sitting room at the B&B. She was wired and could use time to wind down from work. Jason slept soundly in their locked bedroom, and she relished the quiet of the B&B. She kept a baby monitor with her so she could hear if he needed her. That was one good thing about staying here, versus staying in a motel. She'd *never* leave him alone in a motel room, but in Zoe and Nick's house it was like being at home.

She always thought best in silence. As it turned out, Debbie had shown her three homes today, and Jason had actually liked the last one. The house, though a three bedroom and still small, would be perfect for the two of them, plus it had a fenced-in yard and a view of the B&B, which made Jason happy. She still couldn't understand her son's obsession with this house, but at least he liked the little home she'd found. She'd signed the rental agreement, and they would move in tomorrow. She would miss this place, but they required a home of their own.

Her parents would be here with a small moving truck and

all of their personal items. They didn't have much, but at least they'd be sleeping in their own beds tomorrow night.

"Can't sleep?"

She jumped and blinked rapidly, pulling herself from her musings. "Hi, Chris. You're up late."

He eased into the recliner beside the couch. "I'm a night owl and couldn't sleep. I'm used to noise. This place doesn't even have a television to break the silence."

She giggled. "It's funny considering most places have one. Though I haven't missed not having a TV. There is something about this place that makes me content to just be. You know?"

"I suppose so."

She nodded toward a book he'd placed in his lap. "What are you reading?"

He held it up. "The Bible."

Her cheeks burned. She should have recognized it was a Bible. Not that she'd ever read one, but she'd seen the book many times. Her parents even had one on the bookshelf in their house, but they only went to church on Christmas and Easter. "You're a religious person?"

"I don't like to think of myself in those terms. I'm a Christian. I read my Bible, pray, go to church, and try to follow the wisdom found in the Bible. I've found that life is easier to deal with when I keep my relationship close to Him."

"You mean God?"

He nodded. "Do you go to church?"

She shook her head.

"You're welcome to come with me. I found this great little church here on the island. They even have programs for children."

"Thanks, but I don't know." If he knew her past, he might look down on her and regret his invitation. "I should head to bed." She stood and grabbed the baby monitor.

"Don't leave on my account. I'm sick of working and couldn't stare at the four walls in my bedroom any longer. I'd enjoy the company."

"If you're sure." She eased back down, tucked one leg under herself, and made a decision as she did—he didn't need to know her past. "How was the house hunt?"

"Okay. I found a couple of places that are promising, but they're both fixer-uppers."

"You don't want a project?" She couldn't blame him. Construction was expensive on the island since all the materials had to be ferried over.

"Not particularly, but the price is right, and I could make them the way I want, so I'm keeping an open mind."

"Them? I didn't realize you were looking for more than one place."

He shook his head. "It's a duplex. I'd live on one side and rent out the other."

She'd made it clear to her Realtor today that she would not even entertain the idea of living in a duplex. They were all so ugly. "I'm surprised they have those things on the island. Almost everything I've seen here so far has been quaint and aesthetically appealing."

He chuckled. "I take it you don't like duplexes."

"Not particularly. I'm sure there are nice ones out there, but I've yet to see one that had any charm."

"You may be surprised by what I saw today. Keep in mind this is Wildflower and the structures here have their own kind of charm."

She shrugged. He might or might not be right. She'd reserve judgment for now.

He stretched his legs forward, crossing them at his ankles. "How about you? Did you find a place?"

She grinned. "Yes. I was really worried at first since the selection was so low, but Jason loved the last house Deborah showed us. It's within walking distance from here, and you can even see the B&B from the front window."

"Nice. At least you'll have a good view."

She shook her head. "Unfortunately the B&B blocks any view we might have of the Sound, but it's fine. We won't be there forever. My goal is to save enough money to purchase our own home by this time next year."

"Good for you." His eyes warmed. "I've been saving for several years. I'd like to invest in income properties, so I can semi-retire."

"Retire?" She winced at how loud the word came out and lowered her voice. "Sorry, I didn't mean to wake up the entire house. Either you wear your age very well, or you're retiring young."

"*Semi*-retiring, and I am young to retire, but the men in my family don't live past forty-two. I'm in my golden years," he said dryly.

She caught her breath. He was dying? Every instinct in her said to flee. She was drawn to Chris but couldn't get involved with a dying man again. It hurt to lose people. She might have married her husband for the wrong reason and not for love, but she'd cared about him, and it hurt to watch him die.

Chris was suddenly on the couch beside her. He rested a hand on her shoulder. "Hey there, you're as white as the sheets on my bed. Are you okay? Should I wake Nick up? Do you feel like you're going to pass out again?"

"No. I'm fine." The warmth of his hand seared her skin through her sweater. Her heart beat a rapid staccato. He was only worried about her. His touch meant nothing. She took a breath and let it out slowly.

His concerned eyes still studied her, but he pulled his hand away and shifted to a more socially acceptable distance. He remained on the couch. "As long as you're sure."

"I am. If you don't mind my asking, what's wrong with you?" She swallowed the lump that had formed in her throat. If he said he had a brain tumor she was going to burst into tears. She held her breath, afraid to hear his response, but desperate to know.

"Heart disease runs in my family. I've been diagnosed with hypertension."

She let out her breath in a quick puff. "That's hardly a death sentence."

"For the average person you're correct, but my doctor was concerned enough to suggest I change my lifestyle. I'm a driven workaholic, and if I want to live to be an old man, I need to make changes now."

She had no idea how to respond to his statement.

He chuckled. "Hey, you look more upset than me. I'm fine. My blood pressure is down since I've been here, and I've never felt better. I was only joking, well half-joking about being in my golden years. If I follow my doctor's instructions, I could live for many more decades."

She couldn't help but notice his calm acceptance of his situation. If it'd been her, she'd be freaking out and angry. "You seem okay with your prognosis. Why?"

He gave her a half-smile. "It's like this. I've had a lifetime to adjust to the idea that I probably won't live to be an old man, and my faith in the Lord gives me hope. I know when I die that's not the end. I'll get to be in heaven with Him. Granted, I'm in no hurry to get there, hence my lifestyle change, but I'm at peace about my eternity."

"You say the most shocking things, Chris."

He stood and offered her his hand. "How about we call it a night? I don't care to talk about my mortality any more than the next person, and I'm sure I've made you uncomfortable enough for one evening."

She grasped his hand and allowed him to pull her up. "Thanks." She yawned. "It's been a long day, and tomorrow promises to be the same. It's moving day. My parents will be at the rental bright and early with our stuff."

"Could you use any help moving?"

"No thanks. There's not much, and the three of us will have it done in no time." She followed him up the stairs. "'Night,

Chris." They stopped outside her door.

He turned and faced her. "Sleep well, Rachel. And don't worry about what I told you. I can see in your eyes that I've upset you, and I'm sorry for that."

She impulsively stepped forward and wrapped her arms around his waist and gave him a hug. "I'm glad you have your faith, and I'm sorry about your medical condition." As quickly as she'd thrust herself at him, she stepped back and slipped into her bedroom.

Jason lay sound asleep on the bed, his little cheeks a soft pink color in the glow of the bathroom light she'd left on as a nightlight. She quickly readied for bed, desperately trying to push thoughts of Chris from her mind. The man needed someone, but that someone couldn't be her or her son. They'd experienced enough loss, and her heart couldn't take more. But had her heart already become entangled with his?

CHRIS LAY IN BED staring into the darkness. Rachel had surprised him when she'd hugged him. He'd been so startled the best he could muster was a pat on her back as if she were a child. Clearly Rachel was young and impulsive, but he hadn't expected that kind of response to what he'd shared with her this evening.

He still couldn't believe he'd told her about his health and been so open with her about his faith. He never talked about either, except when necessary. Maybe it *had* been necessary. He'd sensed the Lord's hand in that conversation, but that still didn't take away his surprise at his forthrightness with Rachel.

He breathed in deeply, remembering her light citrusy scent and the softness of her hair as it brushed against his cheek. He took a shuddering breath and closed his eyes. She would probably forget about everything he'd told her by morning. He frowned. She'd be leaving the B&B tomorrow. Disappointment hit him. He'd enjoyed visiting with her even if the conversation had turned to a topic he rarely brought up. He'd miss Jason too. The kid was as cute as they come. It was nice having his energy in the B&B. How had he come to look forward to seeing Rachel and her son after only knowing them two days?

CHAPTER SIX

THE DOORBELL PEALED INTO THE QUIET of Rachel's new home.

"I get it!" Jason raced past the kitchen where she had been working since early that morning.

"Wait for me." She yanked off the yellow gloves she wore and rushed to the door. She'd gotten there early to wipe out the cupboards and drawers so when her parents arrived with the moving truck she could put everything away. "Okay. You may open the door now."

With two hands Jason turned the knob and pulled the door toward them. "Granma! Papa!" He lunged at them. "I missed you."

Rachel's dad scooped up her son. "It's good to see you too, Jasie. Have you been a good boy for your mom?"

Jason nodded and hugged her dad's neck. "You live here with us now?"

Dad chuckled softly and peeled his arms from around his neck. "This home is for you and your mom. Isn't that exciting?"

He shrugged. "I like it here, but I miss you."

Rachel stepped forward. If she didn't do something fast,

Jason would end up in an all-out tantrum. "I see you brought our stuff. Jason, all your toys are here." She smiled brightly and took him from her dad's arms. "Go put on your shoes, and you can help."

Jason raced inside.

"Sorry about that. He's been missing both of you."

Her dad gave her a side hug. "We miss the little fellow too, but this is for the best. You both need a fresh start, and from what I've seen of the island this is a good place. Come and grab some boxes. We'll have you settled in no time."

Rachel's mom flitted around the house. "It's small, but cute. I see why you chose this place."

Rachel stood in the center of the living room trying to imagine what her mother saw. The plain white walls and wood floor were in good condition, and the white cabinets in the kitchen directly off the living room looked decent too, but the home was basic vanilla. She'd add pops of color to cheer the place up.

Dad walked in with the frame to Jason's bed. Jason zipped out the door and raced to the truck. "Which box is mine, Mommy?" he shouted the words over his shoulder.

Rachel jogged over to him and found the box that said 'Jason's toys'. "It's probably heavy. Maybe we can carry it inside together."

"Okay." He took one side and she took the other, and in a matter of minutes, Jason hummed happily on one half of his bedroom while her dad put Jason's bed together on the other.

She and her mom worked at bringing in their scant kitchen supplies.

"Your dad and I know how much you've wanted a good set of pots and pans, so we bought you a little house warming present." She pointed to a butcher-paper wrapped box with a green bow on top sitting on the floor. "Go ahead and open it."

Rachel's insides jumped with excitement. "Okay." She knelt and tore away the paper to reveal a beautiful set of stainless cookware. She examined each piece as she removed it. "Oh wow. Thank you. These are perfect." She'd only had a hand-me-down frying pan and pot from her mom's kitchen.

"I didn't bring my old stuff since I knew you'd love these." Mom's smile lit her face.

She and her mom had not always seen eye to eye, and in fact, spent many of her growing up years butting heads, but over the past couple of years, they'd turned a corner and now mostly got along. "This is the best gift. And much needed." She hugged her mom.

Never one for sentimentality Mom quickly brushed her aside. "I suppose we'd best get the rest unloaded and washed up. Moving is tiring business, and I want to help as much as possible before we have to leave." She marched outside and returned with another box.

The rest of the morning flew by in a blur, but by the time her parents left Rachel felt settled, which wasn't difficult since she owned so little. Dad had also surprised her with a washer and dryer. She still couldn't believe they'd spent so much money, but he had said Merry Christmas and happy birthday. She chuckled.

Rachel stood on her front porch and held Jason in her arms as her parents blew kisses from the moving truck.

"Today was fun, Mommy." Jason placed a sloppy kiss on her cheek. "I love you, Mommy, and I love my new room. Can I go play now?"

"Sure." She set him down and waved to her parents as they drove away. A cool breeze lifted her hair off her neck. She ran her hands up and down her arms. This was it—she was officially on her own—officially an adult. With a fleeting look toward her retreating parents, she squared her shoulders and marched inside, closing the door firmly behind her.

"Jason!"

"I in my room," he hollered.

There were three bedrooms in total. Two bedrooms at the

rear of the house with a shared bath between them with a third smaller room at the beginning of the hall. Her bedroom was across the hall from Jason's. One day she'd turn the extra room into a guestroom, but for now it stood empty. The family room and kitchen were at the front with a view of the B&B and trees. It was a shame she couldn't see the Sound from here, but then she would never have been able to afford the place if there was a view.

She meandered down the short hall and stood in the doorway to Jason's room. His red car-shaped toddler bed brightened the otherwise boring room. He sat on the floor building a tower with his blocks. "Look how high it is, Mommy."

"It sure is. How do you like your new room?"

"It's great!"

She tried to envision the room from a three-year-old's perspective and decided he was right. There was plenty of floor space to spread out and play. He didn't have a dresser, but that was fine since most of his stuff could hang, and she could put the rest in easy-to-reach bins in his closet. This place should do fine.

The doorbell rang. "Be right back, Jasie." She rushed to the entryway and pulled open the door. "Zoe! This is a surprise. Come in."

Her boss grinned and held out a covered pot. "I thought you might enjoy a meal you didn't have to prepare yourself. It's a roast. Stick it in the oven, and it'll be ready in time for dinner."

"Thank you!" She took the pot. "Come in." She walked to the kitchen and set the oven to pre-heat.

"I saw your parents leave and wanted to see if you could use any help settling in." Zoe stood in the living room with a slight frown. "Where is all your furniture?"

"In the bedrooms."

"What about the antiques you bought from the B&B a few years ago?"

"Long story short. I ended up selling all of it to a dealer who made me an offer I couldn't refuse."

"Really? I thought for sure that stuff held sentimental value to you."

"At first it did, but after Jason was born, he became more important. I used the money to start a college savings for him."

Zoe raised a brow. "I'm impressed. Good thinking. Oh, before I forget, Nick and I wanted to invite you and Jason to Thanksgiving dinner at our place. We'll have it in our apartment downstairs the day before the holiday. It looks like the restaurant will be open on Thanksgiving, and we'll both be working."

Rachel held back a sigh. Life was so much easier when she had built-in babysitters with her parents. Who would babysit on a holiday? "Thank you for the invite. We'd love to come. What can I bring?"

"I'm glad you asked. I was hoping you'd bring pumpkin pie."

"Sure." They firmed up the time, and she gave Zoe a quick tour. At least the bedrooms were complete.

As they walked into Jason's room, he looked up from the floor where he played. "Hi, Zoe. You want to play?"

"Not today, buddy. But thanks."

"We'll be in the kitchen, Jasie."

"Okay."

She led the way into the only other place in the house that felt homey. Two bar height chairs sat at the island. A Cookie Monster cookie jar sat on the white Corian countertop beside the pantry, and the white refrigerator hummed softly. "Would you like something to drink?" She slid the roast into the oven.

"No thanks. I didn't come over to put you to work. In fact, I'd better head home. Oh, I almost forgot. I removed you from the schedule tonight. I'm sure you and Jason need a night together in your new place for him to feel settled."

Rachel tensed. "Are you sure? What about Piper? After

what happened the other night, I don't want to make any waves."

"I took care of Piper. She understands you were nervous. Don't stress over her. She's a very nice lady and a great boss. She's also a reasonable person so don't worry about taking the night off. Besides, you're not on the schedule anymore. She won't even notice."

Rachel frowned. "I don't like being so easily replaceable."

Zoe chuckled. "If it makes you feel any better, your backup isn't my favorite—that's why I hired you. But he does an adequate job, so don't stress. Everything will be fine as long as we don't have a repeat of your first day. It could have been worse."

Rachel breathed a little easier. "I suppose you're right. I'm thankful the knife only hit a set of stainless steel bowls. I still don't understand how it slipped from my hand. I promise, it won't happen again." What were the chances she'd send a knife flying across a room again? She'd never lost her hold on one before.

"I'm counting on it." Zoe nodded and strode out the door. "I'll see you tomorrow. Be prepared for a busy night. Saturdays are always hopping."

"Okay. Thanks." She waved before closing the door. What was she going to do about Thanksgiving? Maybe Jason could spend the day with her parents. No, that wouldn't work since they were heading out of state to visit friends. The family room, devoid of furniture, made her eyes prick with tears. She took a bracing breath and squared her shoulders. She could handle finding a reliable sitter and furnish her house on an island with no furniture stores and become adept at her new job. She had no choice.

She'd never considered purchasing furnishings online, but in this case it would be the best option. An hour later, she'd placed an order for a couch and loveseat as well as an ottoman, TV, and TV stand and a rug. She paid extra to have it all set up.

Hopefully the stuff would be as comfortable as it looked, and most importantly, fit into her space. She'd had to guess on dimensions since she didn't own a tape measure.

It suddenly occurred to her that she hadn't heard from Jason the entire time she'd been on the Internet. Her stomach dropped, and she hurried to his bedroom. He lay sprawled on his bed, his tattered teddy bear tucked under one arm.

A nap sounded good to her too, but she didn't dare. She slept heavily and couldn't risk that he'd wake before her. A knock on her door caused her to alter course. She pulled the door open, and her heart skipped a beat. "Chris. What brings you by?"

"I was out walking and thinking when Zoe and I crossed paths. She said this is your place and suggested I stop in and say hi."

Why did her excitement at seeing him deflate just because Zoe suggested it? "Jason is sleeping, and I don't have any furniture yet. Maybe we could sit out here on the steps and visit." She pulled the door closed and plopped onto the top stair. Good thing it hadn't rained today, but *brrr* the stairs were cold. Maybe someday she'd buy a bench seat and small table to decorate the front porch, but for now the steps would have to suffice.

"Sounds good to me." He eased down beside her. "I need a second opinion on which direction I should go with my investment, and I was hoping you could help me decide. I thought maybe you and Jason could swing by the places with me."

"Me? Surely you have someone more qualified to ask." Plus they were practically strangers, except it felt like they'd known one another for years. He was easy to talk to.

He chuckled. "Actually, I don't. I've gotten to know you better than anyone else on the island, and it'd be nice to have a friend's opinion."

Friend. Of course they were friends. For whatever reason

they'd hit it off and had spent a decent amount of time together over the past two days, so yes they were friends. "Sure, but I don't know when I'll be able to get away. Jason usually sleeps for about an hour, and I'm not positive when he fell asleep. I was busy ordering furniture online and wasn't paying enough attention to him." She shivered.

"You cold?"

"I should have grabbed my jacket."

He scooted closer until their shoulders touched. "Better?"

Surprisingly it was. "Yes, thanks." Her thoughts rushed to the night before when she'd impulsively hugged him. That was not like her at all, but somehow with him she lost her inhibitions. Clearly he took it as a sign that it was okay to get closer to her, but she wasn't sure it was a good idea to allow him to. She stood. "I'll be right back." She rushed inside and grabbed her jacket out of the entryway closet as well as a green and blue stadium blanket off the shelf.

He looked over his shoulder as she stepped outside. "A blanket? You must really be cold."

She shook her head. "The blanket is to sit on, the coat is to wear." She handed him the blanket, shrugged into her jacket, and stuffed her hands into the pockets. "*Much* better."

He placed the blanket on the top step, then sat and patted the spot beside him. "You were right. It's warmer with a barrier between us and the cold wood."

She sat as far away from him as she could, but still be on the blanket. "I always bring it to football games."

"You like football?" He raised a brow.

"Who doesn't? Besides summer, fall is my favorite time of year. I love the smell in the air, the colder evenings, Friday night games at the high school I graduated from, and best of all, the food."

He chuckled. "That makes sense coming from a chef."

"I make the best pumpkin soup. I'll make you a batch sometime. It's really good."

"I'd like that." His baritone voice soothed her.

The door opened. Jason padded out and wrapped his arms around her neck. "I hungry."

Chris chuckled. "That seems to be a constant state for you."

"I think you're right." She shot him a grin and reached back for her son. "How about we have a snack, then we'll go look at houses."

"We have a house." His bottom lip popped out, and he crossed his arms.

"Chris is house hunting too."

His face brightened. "You like our house?" Her son asked as he plopped onto Chris's lap.

Rachel's eyes widened. What should she do? But from the look on Chris's face he didn't mind.

CHRIS'S INSIDES JOLTED WHEN Jason bounced into his lap. He liked kids, but none had taken to him the way this young one had. It warmed him from head to toe to be accepted by the child. "How about we stop in at the general store for a snack and then go look at houses?"

"Shouldn't you have your Realtor along?"

"Yes, but I saw a listing this morning for a house that intrigues me. I hadn't considered this kind of option, so I hadn't noticed it before. I thought we'd stop by there first, and if I like it from the outside, I'll give him a call. Otherwise he said he'd meet me at the first one he showed me."

"Sounds like fun. Let me grab my purse. I'll drive."

He sent a text to his Realtor to let him know the change in plans. "How do you like your new home, Jason?"

"It's great!" Jason shouted. "But I not sure Mommy likes it."

"Why's that?"

"She cried."

He frowned. Why would Rachel cry? Granted she'd had a rough time of things since she'd been on the island, but not life and death difficult. *Hmm.* She didn't strike him as a crier.

Rachel came back and held out Jason's coat to him.

The child hopped off Chris's lap and quickly slipped into it. He jumped up and down. "I want ice cream." He giggled with a gleam in his eye.

Chris chuckled. "Looks like you have your hands full."

"He's still adjusting to being in a new place. I'm sure he'll settle down once we get into a routine."

He nodded and sat in the front passenger seat while she strapped Jason into his car seat in back. They headed inland. "Take that driveway. There's supposed to be a two-story that's been turned into two separate apartments."

She pulled to a stop in front of a yellow two-story with a wraparound porch and double-door entrance. "Wow. This place is gorgeous."

He couldn't disagree. It was nicer than anything he'd seen yet. "Let me call Jim and get him over here." He pulled out his phone. "The house looks vacant so we could probably walk around while we wait."

"Mom, I still hungry."

Chris wanted to smack his forehead. He'd forgotten the promised snack.

Rachel opened her purse and handed Jason a covered plastic dish. "I turned the oven on low, so the roast will be close to done when we return. Here are some O's for now."

"Thanks." His less than enthusiastic reply made Chris feel bad for forgetting.

Jim answered on the second ring. "I take it you like the place."

"It looks good from the outside. Any chance we can go in?"

"I'll be right there. The house has been on the market over a month and the owners moved out, so if you like the place we could probably get you a deal."

"Sounds good to me. See you in a few." He turned to Rachel. "He's on his way. I have a good feeling about this one."

"I thought you were sold on the duplex idea."

He shook his head. "Not necessarily. One level of this house has been turned into an apartment. I'd still have an income property." Truth be told, her less than enthusiastic response to the idea last night made him table the duplexes, at least for now. Not that he was buying to please her, but he really hadn't been sold on the duplex.

A short time later Jim pulled up, and they all went inside. Chris knew in his gut this was the place.

"The main residence takes up the first and second level, and there is a basement apartment with a private entrance," Jim led them through the house.

"I like the open floor plan," Chris said.

"The basement apartment looks the same as this floor only on a smaller scale since there are two bedrooms."

Thirty minutes later Jason tugged on his sleeve. "I like it here."

He ruffled the boy's hair. "Me too." It looked to be sound and only in need of a new coat of paint and new flooring throughout. Assuming there were no hidden problems like plumbing and electrical, he could handle that if the price was right.

His Realtor ushered them outside and locked up. "Let me know what you decide, Chris."

Chris shook Jim's hand. "Will do." He turned to Jason as his Realtor walked to his vehicle. "How about we go get that ice cream now?"

Rachel bit her bottom lip. "Actually, I'm thinking we should take a rain check. It's getting close to dinner, and I don't want to spoil Jason's appetite." Her face lit as if she had a sudden thought. "Would you like to join us for dinner? I have a roast in the oven and it should be ready in about an hour. I'll pick up ice cream, and we can have it for dessert."

Jason jumped up and down. "Yay!"

How could he say no to that kind of enthusiasm? "I'd like that. It's been a while since I've had a home-cooked meal."

"I'll drop you at the B&B. Dinner will be at six."

He couldn't wait. His stomach rumbled on cue. Jason giggled and slipped his small hand into Chris's. He enjoyed Rachel and her son and couldn't wait for six o'clock.

CHAPTER SEVEN

RACHEL TRIED TO CALM HER NERVES as she poured a cup of decaf for herself and Chris. Her new kitchen wasn't exactly a chef's dream, but it worked and the roast Zoe brought over was melt-in-your-mouth perfect. "Thanks for hanging in there with Jason. I'm sorry he was so difficult tonight. He's really not a bad kid. Most of the time he's like a mini adult."

"He's a three-year-old boy whose life has been in disarray for several days now. Once he gets settled I imagine he'll turn back into the mini adult you know and love." A roguish grin covered his face.

"What, you don't believe me?" She chuckled at his raised brow. "Maybe I was exaggerating a little." She handed him the coffee. "Do you like cream or sugar?"

"Both."

She pulled half and half from the refrigerator. The sugar was already on the counter, so she only needed to grab a spoon. She stood on the other side of the island and sipped the rich roast. "Mmm, this is really good. It's the first time I've tried this brand. Apparently it's a special blend made especially for the café at the general store."

He took a sip of the doctored brew. "Who would have thunk it?" He winked. "A place like this with excellent coffee."

"Hey, you better not be dissing the island. I happen to think very highly of Wildflower." She knew he was teasing, but couldn't help bantering with him. Chris was easy to talk to and made her smile.

He winked before taking another sip. "Why are you standing way over there?" He patted the seat beside him. "Come join me."

She tried to stay calm, but couldn't deny the attraction she had for this man—a very dangerous attraction that she must get over. He was not the man for her. She needed someone who would be around for the long haul. Not some guy who claimed to be in his golden years at the age of thirty-five.

"You never said which place you thought I should buy."

She sat beside him and cradled the mug between her hands on the countertop. "I thought your mind was made up, but I liked the two-story with the basement apartment the best. You already know my thoughts on duplexes, and although those were nicer looking than I'd imagined, the house was pretty special."

His blue eyes studied her through his black-rimmed glasses. "There is something to be said for character. And you're right about the two-story. It oozed character, but what you see as character I see as work. That place is old and probably requires new plumbing and wiring."

"If the price is right what difference does it make?"

"Easy for you to say. You're not the one living in a B&B."

She grinned. "Come on. The Wildflower-Bed-and-Breakfast is the best. I lived there for an entire summer, and Zoe and Nick treated me like family. And believe me when I say I wasn't the perfect guest." She thought back to that summer when she was trying to figure out what to do about being a pregnant widow. She'd had little money and no idea what to do with her life, much less how to raise a baby she wasn't sure she wanted. But that summer had changed things.

Zoe in particular had made the biggest impact on her. She hadn't judged her for the situation she found herself in and she tried her best to help her and include her in the everyday life around the B&B even though she didn't deserve it.

"Tell me about that summer. I know you've told me some, but you said there was more."

"True, but some things are best left to the imagination." She shot him a wicked grin and laughed when his eyes widened. "You never answered *my* question. Did you make a decision about which house to buy?"

"I think so. In spite of what I said about the place, I'll put in an offer on the two-story with the condition of a home inspection. I'm open to doing some minor renovation, but not a ton."

"Good for you." She yawned. "Tonight's been fun. Thanks for coming over."

He stood. "And that's my cue to leave. Sorry, I spend more time with computers than people and my social graces are inept."

Her stomach fluttered at the embarrassment she read on his face. "Not at all." She rested a hand on his arm. "I'm used to staying up late, but figured you would be getting bored with my company by now." She removed her hand from his arm.

"Not even." He looked toward her living room. "I'd suggest we move to more comfortable seating, but it looks like this is it."

She grinned at the teasing in his voice. "I paid for expedited shipping so it will be here next week. I'd invite you over to assemble it all, but I paid extra for that too." She didn't like that it had cost her more, but overall it was cheaper than going to a furniture store on the mainland and paying for delivery. And it was a *lot* faster since she didn't have to drive from store to store looking for what she liked. She envisioned where her furniture would go and Chris sitting there with her. *Stop.* She couldn't keep going there.

He moved toward the entryway. "I hope you'll invite me back once this place is put together."

"Of course. You're welcome here anytime, but after today, my evenings will be filled. Which reminds me, I still have to find a sitter for Thanksgiving."

"Really? Will your furniture be here by then?"

"Yes."

"Will you have a TV?"

She had a feeling where this conversation was going and grinned. "As a matter of fact I will. And as you know I'm a sports fan, so I'll have ESPN too."

"Hmm. I happen to be free for Thanksgiving."

"What, no family or girlfriends to entertain?"

"OH, I HAVE FAMILY, but no girlfriends." He seriously enjoyed this evening and wished it could go longer. Rachel was fun, and he was dreading spending the holiday at the B&B with no television to watch the game. "My family doesn't do anything together for Thanksgiving, so if you don't mind a *man* watching him I'd be happy to watch Jason."

"Ah yes, my comment about Jason not being used to men is coming back to bite me. I'd be very comfortable with you watching him. He likes you. And so do I."

Rachel's face glowed, igniting something in him he thought long dead. He wanted to see her smile like that all the time.

"Good. Because I like the both of you too, and I'd be happy to spend the day with Jason."

"Thank you." She pulled him into a bear hug. "You are like my guardian angel or something. Every time I turn around you're getting me out of a tough situation."

This time he didn't freeze up at her gregarious behavior. He wrapped his arms around her, breathed in her citrus scent, and held her there for a moment before releasing her. "I'll take that as yes. What time should I be here?"

"Is ten too early?"

"No. But I wasn't expecting you to need me that early in the day. Do you mind if I bring my computer and work while I'm here?"

"Not at all, so long as you keep an eye on Jason."

His heart thudded as he looked into her trusting brown eyes. He cleared his throat and stepped back. He was treading on dangerous ground. Rachel didn't share his faith and that made her off limits. "I should go. I'll let you know what happens with the house."

"Good luck. I hope it works out for you," she said at the door as he walked down the steps to the driveway. He turned and waved to the raven-haired beauty. He headed to the B&B. Rachel was young and sweet, but sadness and an air of vulnerability surrounded her. He would enjoy figuring out the cause. He always enjoyed a good mystery. And Rachel was definitely worth investigating.

CHAPTER EIGHT

THANKSGIVING MORNING CHRIS KNOCKED ON RACHEL'S front door. He hadn't seen much of her since he'd been busy working and dealing with house stuff. He would close on the two-story in two weeks.

"You're here!" Rachel moved aside. "Thanks for coming a little early. I have turkey in the fridge along with all the trimmings. All you do is reheat and eat."

"Whoa. Slow down, Rachel."

She stopped and turned, her brows bunched in obvious confusion. "What?"

"I'm fine. And Happy Thanksgiving."

A slow grin raised her mouth. "Sorry. I'm in sonic speed mode trying to get everything done before I have to leave."

"What can I do to help?"

"Watch the parade with Jason."

Her son lay on his belly on top of an oversized red and brown ottoman, resting his chin on his hands. He rolled over. "Hi, Chris!"

Chris sat on the couch facing the television. "Hey there, buddy. How're you doing?"

"Grrr-ate! Mommy made Thanksgiving for us. I can't wait! We had it at Zoe and Nick's too." He patted his stomach. "Mommy says I'm going to turn into stuffing." He giggled.

Chris glanced toward the hall where Rachel had disappeared. "It sounds like your mom has been very busy. Have you been a good helper?"

"Yep. I tore bread for dressing, and I helped make pumpkin pie."

"My favorite."

Rachel rushed into the room. "Chris, will you come into the kitchen for a minute? I have things to go over with you."

"Sure. Be right back, buddy."

Jason nodded and resumed his position watching the parade.

"What's up?"

She handed him a piece of paper. "If you have an emergency, here's my cell number and the restaurant's number in case you can't reach me. Like I said, all the food is in the fridge. Help yourself to whatever you want. Jason should be in bed by eight and no later. He will try to talk you into letting him stay up, but don't." She relayed the instructions to him then paused, tapping her list with a pen. "I feel like I'm forgetting something."

"Relax, Rachel. I've got this. Jason and I are going to have a great day."

"Oh, I know what it is." She lowered her voice and leaned close. "He's regressed with potty training. You'll have to remind him every hour to go to the bathroom."

"Every hour?"

"Yes. Unless you want to risk an accident."

He raised his hand. "No, ma'am. Every hour it is."

"Good. I can't thank you enough for today."

He placed a hand on each of her shoulders. "Look at me, Rachel."

Her gaze darted to his and locked. She was wound up as

tight as a toy soldier.

"Breathe. Everything will be okay. Jason and I get along very well, and I've been looking forward to this day all week."

She visibly relaxed and chuckled. "You've probably been dreaming about watching football."

He grinned and released her arms. "As a matter of fact, I have."

She took a breath and let it out in a short puff. "Okay. I trust you. And I know Jason is excited to have you here. But promise me you'll call if there is a problem."

"Promise."

She hugged him then launched into the family room. He wasn't sure if he'd ever get used to her hugs, but clearly she didn't mean anything romantic by them. In a funny way, she reminded him of the character who played Abby on NCIS when it came to hugging.

Rachel planted a kiss on her son's head, mouthed thank you to Chris, then darted out the door. Hopefully she'd calm down, or he might be making another trip to the hospital to pick her up.

He sat back on the couch and looked around. She'd done a nice job creating a homey environment for herself and her son. The two-tone couch and love seat had a leather base with red cushions. The area rug was a neutral shade with pops of red, and the TV, though on the small side, fit the space nicely. He leaned back with his fingers laced behind his head and propped his feet on the ottoman.

Jason lifted his head and looked at him. "Can we get a tree today?"

"A Christmas tree?" It looked like the parade had put the boy in the holiday spirit.

"Yeah."

"I don't think so, little dude. Your mom will want to do that with you."

"We surprise her." Jason looked at him with puppy dog

eyes. He was good at this begging thing.

"Are you getting hungry?" Maybe distraction would work.

The boy hopped off the ottoman and ran to the kitchen. "Cookies!"

He chuckled and followed slowly. This day was going to be a lot longer than he'd imagined. A clunking sound from the back of the house drew his attention. "Hold on a second, Jason." He left the boy alone and moved toward the back of the house.

The clunking got louder, then a scream inside the house rang out.

RACHEL JULIENNED A RED pepper. So far things were going well. Her co-workers were in a good mood and the vibe in the kitchen was pleasant. After her rocky first night, she had wondered if she'd made a mistake taking this job, but now she knew it was where she belonged.

Piper walked into the kitchen holding a phone to her ear, an expression of concern on her face. She looked around the room and her gaze landed on Rachel.

Rachel's stomach flipped, and her heart thudded. "What's wrong?" She put down the knife she'd been using and rushed to Piper. "Is it Jason?"

She pulled it away and covered the receiver with her hand. "No, it's Chris. He needs to talk with you. You may want to take this someplace more private." Piper thrust the phone into her outstretched hand.

Alarm shot through her, and her feet felt like lead. "Chris, it's Rachel. What's wrong?"

"Nothing too serious, but I'm at the hospital with Jason."

"What?"

The sounds of the kitchen faded. Everyone stared at her. She lowered her voice and moved into the walk-in pantry, shutting the door behind her. "What happened and who is hurt? You or Jason?"

"It's Jason. He fell off the kitchen counter and hurt his arm."

She closed her eyes telling herself not to overreact. *Breathe in and out.* "I'll be there as soon as I can."

"Okay, but for now I need you to talk with someone here and tell them it's okay to treat Jason. Since his injury is not life threatening, they need your permission."

"Pass the phone over, then I want to talk with you, so don't hang up." She couldn't believe this was happening. She should have known better than to leave her son with a man. She gave her permission for Jason to be treated, then Chris's voice came back on the line. "What happened?"

A knock sounded on the pantry door. She poked her head out. Piper stood there. "I'm really sorry, but I need my phone back."

"Oh." Of course Piper would need her phone. It's how everyone at the resort reached her, and she was tying up the line. "Chris, I'll need to call you back."

"Okay. I tried your cell phone first, so you have my number."

"Thanks." She pressed the end button and walked back into the kitchen. All eyes were trained on her. She returned the phone to Piper. "Sorry about that."

"It wasn't a problem. Will your son be okay?" Piper asked. Concern clouded her eyes.

"I think so. I still don't know what happened. I had to give the hospital permission to treat him." She walked over to Zoe. "Can I take a break and call Chris back, so I know what's going on?"

"Of course. Do you need to go to the hospital?"

"I'd like to, but how will you manage here?"

"We will all work a little faster until you return."

"Okay. I'll hurry." Rather than waste time calling Chris back, she grabbed her purse and fled out the back door that led to employee parking. Going to the hospital was becoming way too common an occurrence. She sped along the near empty road to the hospital, parked and ran inside. She looked around the room and spotted the receptionist. "Excuse me, my son is here. May I join him?"

"Of course. Who is your son?"

She told her, and a moment later the woman clicked something that allowed the door to the treatment area to open. "Thank you." She rushed through the doorway and immediately heard her son. Following his voice she found him behind the first curtain. "Hey, buddy."

He sat on the exam table holding an ice pack on his arm. His puffy red eyes spoke volumes. She went to him and rubbed his back. "What happened?"

"I wanted a cookie and fell."

She looked at Chris for an explanation.

"We were in the kitchen and going to get a snack when I heard a clunking sound at the back of the house."

Water pipes. Those things were awful. If she'd known the racket they made, she never would have signed the lease.

"I was only gone a minute, and the next thing I know, Jason screams. He'd climbed on to the counter and slipped, landing on his arm."

Her heart rate finally began to slow, and she realized her legs shook. She turned to her son. "I've told you not to climb onto the counter because you could fall and get hurt."

Jason's eyes watered. "I sorry." Silent tears streamed down his face, breaking her heart.

"Me too, buddy." She wanted to hug him, but didn't want to cause him pain. She continued to rub his back, swallowing her own tears. "I'm sorry about this Chris. You'll never want to babysit again."

He shrugged, clearly too polite to deny the truth.

The curtain slid open, and a man wearing scrubs walked in. "Ms. Narrelli?"

"Yes." She nodded.

"The business office asked me to make sure you filled out this paperwork. We already have you in our records but must have the part regarding your son filled out."

"Of course. Thank you." She took the pen he offered and sat down. Her hand shook as she filled in the form then signed a shaky version of her signature.

Jason rested on the exam bed quietly and watched the TV that had been tuned into the football game. She glanced at Chris and noted his eyes were glued to the screen. At least he hadn't missed all of his game.

Jason seemed content as long as he sat still. "How you doing, Jasie?"

"Okay. My arm hurts." Crocodile tears slipped down his cheek causing her own eyes to water. She blinked away the threatening tears and cleared her throat.

Glancing at her watch, she sighed. A good thirty minutes had passed watching the game with the guys and waiting for a doctor, but she couldn't wait any longer. Zoe expected her to return to the restaurant. "The restaurant is expected to be super busy today, and I need to go back to work. Will the two of you be okay together?" She looked at Chris, who nodded, then Jason, who did as well.

"Thank you for being such a big boy, Jason. Please listen to Chris today and no more climbing onto counters." She brushed the hair off his forehead and gave him a kiss. "Will you call me when you know if it's broken or not?" Although from looking at it, she highly doubted he had broken his arm. She suspected a sprain at the most.

"Of course. You can't stay a little longer?" Chris asked.

She checked the time again. "If I hadn't gotten off to such a rocky start at the restaurant, I wouldn't go back." It was clear Jason was comfortable with Chris. "How long do you think it will take?"

"The nurse said an orderly will be coming in soon to take

him to x-ray."

She nodded. "Don't leave him, Chris. Please go with him to x-ray."

"I will."

"Thanks. I owe you." She moved to pass him so she could exit the cubicle, but he caught her hand.

"He's going to be okay." Chris's intense eyes held a promise of hope.

"I know. Or I wouldn't leave. Even if it meant losing my job. Thank you for being here with him."

He nodded and released her hand.

An orderly came in wearing a big smile. "You must be Jason." The woman who looked to be in her fifties spoke gently to her son. "How would you like to go for a ride in this wheelchair?"

Jason's eyes brightened, and he nodded.

Chris stood and helped her son off the bed and settled him into the wheelchair. Jason looked at the man with adoration in his eyes. She could understand that feeling. Chris was a special man.

Confident that her son was in good hands, Rachel did one of the hardest things she ever had to do and left. The rest of the work day flew by in a blur.

At the end of the evening Zoe stopped her on the way out. "Thanks for coming back today. You did a great job, and I'm glad Jason wasn't badly hurt."

"Me too. A sprain is so much better than a break. He has to wear a brace for a while, but that's not too big a deal. Especially this time of year." She waved then headed to her car and ten minutes later pulled into her driveway. The lights inside shone brightly, casting a glow onto the front porch.

She strode to the door and let herself in. Chris sat on the couch, his computer by his side with Jason's head on his lap. By the look of her son, he was sound asleep. A brace covered his left arm and an icepack sat on the ottoman. Chris's hand rested on her son's back.

The television played *It's a Wonderful Life*. She moved his computer aside and eased down beside him. "How'd it go?" She kept her voice low, so Jason wouldn't wake.

"Smooth as the delicious pumpkin silk pie you left for us." He whispered back. "We were watching football when he fell asleep. I didn't want to disturb him by taking him to bed. He had Tylenol at six for the pain. He's wearing a compression bandage to help reduce swelling. You'll want to ice his arm tomorrow, but after that use heat for short periods of time if it's achy. The doctor also suggested elevating his arm with a pillow. He seems to be doing okay."

"That's a relief. I worried about him all day."

"He has a bad sprain. The doctor thinks it could take three or four weeks to heal."

Her shoulders sagged. She'd hoped a sprain wouldn't be such a big deal and he'd be fine by Christmas. "I imagine you're sore from sitting there so long. I'll carry Jason to bed and be right back." She stood, walked around the ottoman, then hefted her son into her arms, careful to avoid bumping his arm.

He snuggled into her. "Hi, Mom." His eyes drooped. "We had fun, but my arm hurts."

"I know, kiddo. I'm sorry." She went into his room, pulled back the covers with one hand, then placed him on the cool sheets and covered him to his chin. Before leaving the room, she clicked on his nightlight then closed the door behind her.

Chris patted the spot beside him when she walked into the family room. "What a day."

She eased onto the couch and twisted to face him. "I'm really sorry about Jason."

"I'm the one who should apologize. He got hurt on my watch. Incidentally, I think your landlord should have the plumbing looked at. It makes some odd sounds."

"You're right. Sorry about that, too." Why was she always such a mess?

"Don't be sorry. It's not your fault the plumbing here needs help. Come here, you look like you could use a shoulder rub."

"Anyone ever tell you you're a nice guy?" She scooted closer and turned her back to him. His gentle fingers kneaded the tired and sore muscles in her neck and shoulders.

"Maybe. How's that feel?"

"Wonderful." She closed her eyes and allowed her head to dip forward. "You could do this for a living."

He chuckled.

"I'm serious." She turned, causing him to drop his hands. "I should be offering to rub your shoulders after the day you had."

He shrugged. "It really wasn't that bad. It's not a day I'd care to repeat, but it could have been much worse."

"That's one way to look at it." She really liked this man.

"I should go." He stood. "Thanks for the meal. You didn't have to go to so much trouble."

Disappointment hit her. She wanted him to stay, but it was late, and he was probably as worn out as she was. "It was my way of saying thank you for watching Jason today. I'm sure you could've found a TV to watch the game on without having to spend several hours at the hospital and playing with my son for half the day."

He chuckled, the truth of her words in his eyes. "For what it's worth, Rachel, in spite of everything, I enjoyed myself. It was nice being here, and it brought back a lot of good memories. So thank you."

She looked into his eyes and nodded, wishing things were different. Her heart was already entangled with his, and she wanted him to be a part of their lives on a much deeper level than just as a good friend.

He gently touched her cheek with the palm of his hand. Her eyes widened and her breath hitched.

"You are a very special lady, Rachel. Rest well." He dropped his hand and walked out the door.

Disappointment washed over her as she watched him walk away, taking a piece of her heart with him. How had she fallen for him so fast, and what was she going to do about it?

IT TOOK EVERY OUNCE of willpower to walk out Rachel's door without kissing her. She drew him like no other woman ever had. But the way things stood now, anything more than friendship was impossible. He prayed daily that she would come to a saving faith in the Lord.

He ran a hand down his face as he sat behind the wheel of his car looking back at her little house. Rachel and Jason would make some man very happy one day. He started up the car and headed to the B&B.

Jason was such a cute kid. He hoped to have a boy like him in the future, but would a woman even want him given his family history with heart disease and the men in his family dying so young?

It's not like he'd been required to disclose that information. His doctor said his heart, though not as healthy as it could be, looked pretty good all things considered. But Chris couldn't help being a pessimist, considering his family history.

He was lonely and wanted a family. If that was ever going to happen he must stop thinking about the condition of his heart and start looking for the right woman. One who was willing to take life as it came and accept the good with the bad. He already knew Rachel could do that, but he couldn't put her through losing a spouse again. Nor could he consider dating her if they didn't have the same beliefs. His faith was everything to him.

CHAPTER NINE

RACHEL STOOD AT THE KITCHEN COUNTER at the Wildflower Bed-and-Breakfast. She'd stopped in for a cup of coffee, but Zoe was busy making Christmas cut-out cookies, so Rachel decided to roll up her sleeves and help. Jason was downstairs with Nick and his nephew Aiden, who was visiting for the weekend.

"We could use more star cookies, Rachel." Zoe handed her the cookie cutter, then pulled a tray from the oven. "Perfect." She grinned and set the tray on a wire rack. "How are you and Jason adjusting to life on the island?"

"It's been rough at times, but all things considered, the transition has gone well."

"Good." She motioned toward a set of cookie cutters. "Those are for the nativity scene. I want to make a display in the entryway."

Rachel wanted to ask Zoe about her faith but didn't know how to bring it up. Ever since Chris had stated he was a Christian and invited her to church, she hadn't been able to get his faith from her mind. He was a good guy, better than most, and she admired Zoe and Nick. They all had their faith in common. Was she missing out on something special by not believing the way they did?

It wasn't like she had anything against God. She'd never given Him much thought—even when she was pregnant and trying to decide what to do. She never would have terminated her pregnancy, but she'd seriously considered giving her baby up for adoption. Considering everything else she'd put her parents through, she'd been so afraid of how they would respond when they found out she had not only been married, but was with child.

As it turned out they were cool about it. They hadn't been happy to learn she'd married and not told them, or that her husband had died, or that she'd only married him because she was pregnant, but they had insisted she move back in with them. They had even supported her and watched Jason while she went to culinary school. She couldn't have asked for more.

Rachel pressed the star into the last empty space on the dough. She wanted to be a good mom for Jason. Was she being neglectful by not taking him to church? "Do you and Nick go to a church here on the island?"

"Yes. There are actually a couple of different ones, but we like Wildflower Community Church near the golf club."

"I've seen that place. It looks like a historic building with the spire."

Zoe grinned. "I imagine it is historic. The people there are nice, the preaching is good, and I especially like the worship. It's a good mix of contemporary songs with hymns."

"So you sing there?" Rachel had heard her friend sing, and it wasn't pretty.

"Absolutely. That's the best part to my way of thinking. You should come sometime. There's a great children's program. I imagine Jason would have fun being around other kids his age."

"Do a lot of kids go there?" One of the downfalls of moving to the island was the lack of playmates for her son. He'd already spent too much time around adults, but it was worse here.

"Not really, maybe three or four at the most, but that's better than none."

Rachel nodded. "Will you text me the details? I may check it out."

"Sure. If you decide to come, let me know, and I'll save you a spot beside us."

"Thanks."

A commotion came from the direction of the downstairs apartment, and the kids burst into the kitchen. Aiden and Jason were laughing.

"What's so funny?" Rachel rolled out a new slab of dough.

"Aiden tells funny jokes." Her son stuck his nose up and sniffed. "Cookies!"

Zoe chuckled. "That's right. If your mom says it's okay you may have one."

"Sure. Go wash your hands first."

The boys rushed to the sink. She couldn't believe how much Aiden had grown in only three years. The last time she'd seen him he'd been five. It was hard to believe he was eight already.

Rachel wondered at how different Zoe was from the summer when she stayed here. The woman was more relaxed now and seemed comfortable in her own skin. "I heard that we might have snow for Christmas this year."

Jason squealed. "Snow! I love snow."

Rachel laughed and handed each boy a cookie. Her son had never even seen snow in real life.

Nick stepped into the kitchen from the downstairs apartment. "Now don't get the kids all excited about something that may or may not happen. We haven't seen one flake in the three years we've been here. Plus Christmas is several weeks away, and there's no way to predict with accuracy that far out."

"Ha." Zoe barked. "They get it wrong with a ten-hour lead-time. But I hope the prediction is right. It would be fun to have a white Christmas. Which reminds me, Rachel. The resort books sleigh rides Friday through Sunday. Well, pseudo sleigh rides. The sleigh has wheels that can be taken off in case it actually snows. You and Jason should go on a ride. The resort is really beautiful at night now since Chase has all the lights up on the property. Come to think of it, you should check out all the activities the resort offers. It's quite the lineup."

"Thanks. I'll look into it. I've always been a fan of Christmas lights."

"Too bad you missed the tree lighting in the park connected to the hospital. It's really something. Someone donated a gazebo to the town and had it placed there. It's beautiful this time of year."

"It sounds like Wildflower Island is the place to be at Christmas time. I didn't realize there was so much going on."

"You don't know the half of it," Nick said. "This place is sure to put almost anyone in the Christmas spirit. Now that Thanksgiving is past, wait and see."

Zoe pulled a pan of cookies from the oven and slid another one in. "He's right. In fact, as we speak, Piper has a team decking out the restaurant. It's quite the transformation."

"It sure seems like a lot of work for only a few weeks."

"The best few weeks ever," Aiden piped in.

"Hello." The kitchen door swung forward, and Chris poked his head in. "Sorry to interrupt, but it sounds like you're having too much fun."

Rachel's insides warmed at the sight of Chris. She hadn't seen or heard from him since Thanksgiving, two days ago when she thought for sure he was going to kiss her.

"Hey, Chris," Nick said. "Come in and join us."

"Have a cookie and tell me what you think." Zoe slid a platter of unfrosted cookies toward him.

"Thanks." He took a bite. "They're good, but there's something different about them."

"I use almond extract instead of vanilla. I like to surprise the senses."

He popped the rest of the star shaped cookie into his mouth.

Jason tugged on Chris's pant leg with his good arm. "Can you come and play at my house again?"

Rachel's heart was about to burst. The timer, the loudest noise in the room, sounded like a grandfather clock in the silence following her son's question.

CHRIS SQUATTED TO JASON'S LEVEL. "I don't know, buddy. That's up to your mom." He looked up at Rachel, who had a perplexed look on her face. If only he could read her mind.

"You're welcome any time, Chris."

"Okay." He stood. "Thanks." The warmth in her gaze almost sent him reeling. This was getting complicated. No, they were just friends.

Nick cleared his throat breaking the tension in the room. "The resort is playing *Elf* tonight out on the green. Actually they play a movie every Saturday during the month of December. They do a bonfire and make s'mores. There's plenty of hot chocolate to go around. Everyone brings blankets and sits on the grass."

"Brr," Rachel said. "It's freezing outside, even with a bonfire."

Perfect snuggling weather. Chris shook the thought away.

"As long as it's dry it's pretty fun. Zoe and I went last year." Nick broke a cookie and popped half into his mouth.

"You actually had a weekend night off?" Rachel was surprised Zoe would allow anyone else to run her kitchen on a busy weekend.

"Piper thought it was important that Nick and I enjoy the festivities. We went on a sleigh ride after the movie. It was cold, but fun."

"Sounds like it." Rachel looked toward Jason. "Would you

like to do that sometime?"

His eyes widened. "Yes!"

"You have next Saturday off, Rachel. You should plan to go."

Rachel's gaze slammed into Chris's. "Would you like to join us?"

More than anything. But the more time they spent together the more he wanted to be with her, and that wasn't fair to either of them. "Thanks, but I have plans."

Disappointment shone briefly in her eyes before it disappeared, and she plastered on a smile. "Okay. Looks like it's me and you, Jasie."

He felt like a world class jerk for saying he couldn't be there, but it was the truth—sort of. He'd tentatively volunteered to help at the missionary banquet the church he'd been attending was holding on Saturday night. He hadn't said he'd be there for sure, but he would now. Being new there, he figured volunteering would be a good way to get to know people.

Jason gave him a hangdog look that about broke his resolve to distance himself from the little family that drew him so strongly. He averted his eyes from the boy. "I guess I should be going." He headed for the kitchen door that led to the dining room.

"Hold up a minute." Nick's long stride easily caught up to him at the stairs. "What was that all about?"

Chris glanced toward the room he'd fled and lowered his voice. "I don't know what you mean."

Nick crossed his arms and gave him a look that tightened his gut. "Rachel is nice. What's the deal with snubbing her like that?"

"I wasn't snubbing her. I really have something else going on." Where did Nick get off challenging him?

"But you like her." Nick's stance had relaxed, but suspicion still filled his eyes.

"Yes. Very much, but it doesn't matter because she is off

limits."

Nick glanced toward the kitchen, grabbed his arm, and dragged him outside to the porch.

"It's freezing out here."

"Too bad. I think of Rachel like a kid sister, even if I haven't seen or heard from her in over three years. Why is she off limits?"

"She's not a Christian. I feel strongly that for a relationship to work, both individuals must believe the same way. I don't have any desire to be involved in a relationship that is doomed before it even begins, no matter how much I like her."

Nick's shoulders sagged. "I hadn't thought of that. But you're right. Actually I think the Bible talks about that too."

"Yes. It's found in 2 Corinthians 6:14."

"You know your Bible well."

Chris shrugged.

Nick frowned. "I never gave Rachel's spiritual life any thought. That's about to change. Out of curiosity what are you doing Saturday?"

"There's a thing at church."

Nick nodded as if he knew exactly what Chris was talking about. "I'll cover for you. That way you could see the movie with Rachel and Jason. I know she'd appreciate the company. Watching a movie together doesn't mean you have to marry her."

Chris laughed. "You don't get it. I like her—a lot. The more time I spend with her the harder it is not to fall for her."

Nick sighed. "When you put it like that, I see the problem."

Chris felt cold to his bones. His teeth chattered. "You think we could go inside now?"

"Yeah, sorry. It feels like it's going to snow." Nick opened the door and warm air gushed out.

"Thanks. Don't say the S word."

Nick laughed. "Not a fan of snow?"

"Not a fan of the mess it makes on the roads. It's nice to look at while sitting by a fire."

Nick nodded. "True enough."

Chris jogged up the stairs to his room. Maybe he was approaching this Rachel thing all wrong. After all, there was no harm in being friends with her. He simply wouldn't fall in love with her. No harm no foul as they say. But he already said he couldn't do the movie, so he'd better call the church and let them know he would be there.

He reached for his cell phone to call his contact at church. "Is this Ray?"

"Yes."

Chris introduced himself. "I wanted you to know that I'm free to help at the banquet on Saturday."

"Thanks, but I wasn't sure you'd be able to since you hadn't gotten back to me, so I found someone else. Maybe next time."

"There's nothing you need help with?"

"Nada. Everyone really stepped up. Our church is very missions-oriented."

"Okay. Sorry I didn't get back to you sooner. Take it easy." He disconnected the call. He'd never heard of a church turning down a volunteer, but there was a first time for everything. Now what?

His conscience ate at him. He paced to the window that looked onto the Sound and suddenly knew what he would do. Before he could talk himself out of it, he yanked open his bedroom door and trotted down the stairs.

Jason's voice rose loudly from the kitchen. It sounded like the kid was having a meltdown. Maybe now wasn't such a good time. He hesitated at the bottom step. Then again he might be able to help with Jason. The boy liked him, and other than the mishap in the kitchen and subsequent trip to the hospital on Thanksgiving, they'd had a decent time together.

He squared his shoulders and marched into the kitchen, once again ignoring the do-not-enter sign. "What's this I hear?" He sought out Jason, who sprawled on the floor, with tears streaming down the sides of his face.

"Mommy said we had to leave."

"Well, buddy. If that's what your mom said, what are you doing lying on the floor?" He offered the boy a hand up, and to his relief Jason grasped it and stood. "Would you like a ride on my shoulders to your car?"

"Put your coat on, Jasie." Rachel stepped forward with his jacket.

The boy quickly complied then turned around so Chris could hoist him onto his shoulders. "Duck on the way out the door."

"I know. Come on, Mommy," he said excitedly.

Rachel slipped into her jacket and walked beside him. "What are you up to?"

"Nothing. But as it turns out I'm free on Saturday after all. If the offer still stands, I'd like to join you and Jason for the movie Saturday."

"And the sleigh ride?"

The excitement in Jason's voice made him chuckle. "Yes, buddy. The sleigh ride too, but make sure you both bundle up."

"No kidding." Rachel opened the passenger door on the driver's side. "It's really cold during the day, so I can only imagine how cold it will be after dark. So you really had plans?" She eyed him skeptically.

"Tentative, but they fell through. I'm glad I caught the two of you before you left."

"It's not like we live far." She pointed to her house, which could barely be seen through a stand of trees.

"True enough." It was weird how she could see the B&B from her place, but the view from the B&B to her place wasn't great. He swung Jason down.

"That was fun. Thanks, Chris." Jason hugged his leg, then climbed into the backseat.

Chris's heart melted a little. He was in big trouble when it came to Jason and his mom. Staying only friends would not be easy with the boy tugging at his heartstrings without even trying. At least Rachel seemed oblivious to the effect she and her son had on him. He prayed it stayed that way, and that his heart would behave as well.

CHAPTER TEN

RACHEL SIPPED TEA WHILE CURLED UP on the sofa in her living room. Jason finally napped in his bedroom. She took a deep breath and let it out slowly, hoping it would relieve the tension in her shoulders.

Jason had been crabby and difficult all day. It was days like today she hated being a single mom and missed living with her parents, even though the entire time she was there, she couldn't wait to move out. It's funny how the things you think you want the most, end up being the things you like the least. Being independent with absolutely no support system in place was difficult.

Now that Jason was sleeping, maybe she had time for a bubble bath. It was worth a try. She could take the baby monitor in there with her in case he woke up early. A bottle of lavender scented bath salts sat on the counter. She poured a liberal amount as hot water rushed into the old-fashioned claw foot tub, and breathed in deeply her favorite scent. There was something about the aroma of lavender that made her happy. A few minutes later she eased into the water and closed her eyes. This was exactly what she needed.

She'd been looking forward to movie night at the resort ever since Zoe suggested it. Jason was beside himself with excitement, which was more than likely another reason he'd been out of control today.

Tonight should be fun. Since Chris said he was free to join them, she'd reserved a sleigh ride for the three of them after the movie ended. Chris confused her. When he said he'd had plans she thought for sure he was trying to blow her off, which hurt. They got along well and even if there could never be a future for them romantically, she'd like to count him as a friend.

The more she thought about keeping him in friend status the more she questioned herself. What kind of person wouldn't consider a future with someone simply because he said he would die young? Well, maybe not in so many words, but it was implied. She'd heard of many cases where doctors had been wrong and their patients had gone on to live well beyond their predictions.

Why did he have to be such a great guy, and why did Jason have to adore him? Maybe she should at least be open to the idea of dating Chris because she really wanted to in spite of everything. She sighed—he'd have to ask her out first. She could never bring herself to ask him on a real date—a movie with herself and her son didn't count. Maybe she'd read him wrong, and he wasn't even interested. She couldn't humiliate herself like that. This was a small island, and they were sure to bump into one another from time to time. It could be awkward if things didn't work out.

Her thoughts drifted to the evening ahead. She was a little concerned about the weather. It was cold, as December should be, and it seemed unhealthy to sit outside to watch a movie. Then again, there would be propane heaters and a bonfire for making s'mores. Jason would be bundled from head to toe for certain.

Rustling sounded from the monitor—her cue to get out. She rushed to dry off and slipped into a fluffy robe. After poking her head into Jason's bedroom and seeing he was still asleep, but restless, she scooted into her room and slipped into jeans and a red sweater.

"Mommy." Her bedroom door swung open. Jason stood there rubbing his eyes. "I'm hungry."

"You're always hungry. And please knock and wait for me to tell you to come in."

"Sorry." He turned and darted off.

She had a simple meal of bean and vegetable soup and bread planned. Chris would be joining them since the B&B didn't serve dinner. She'd had the soup simmering much of the day and the aroma of veggies, spices and broth permeated the house. It should be perfect by the time he arrived for an early dinner. The movie started at six since the event was designed for families.

She followed her son into his bedroom and laid out what she wanted him to change into after their meal. "Remember, Chris is coming for dinner, and I expect you to be on your best behavior."

"I know. I be good. When are Granma and Papa coming? Will they be here for Christmas? I miss them." This move had been difficult on Jason. Accustomed to being with her parents, he'd been acting out with tantrums.

"I don't think so, Jasie. Grandma and Papa have lots of travel plans." She hadn't realized how much her parents had put their lives on hold to help raise Jason while she lived with them for the past three years. They were probably so excited to have their freedom they hadn't even considered Christmas. She wouldn't hold it against them. Creating her own traditions with her son would be nice.

"I want a Christmas tree." Jason sat beside his bed playing with a car, one arm still in a sling.

Rachel sucked in her bottom lip. She needed to hurry up and buy a tree. The holiday would be past before she had it up, and then her son would be disappointed. "What if we go get one tomorrow?"

Jason jumped up and down. "Yay! I want a star."

"A star for the top is a good idea. Maybe we can make one."

"With glitter?"

She hesitated. Glitter made such a mess. "How about gold paint?"

Jason raised his shoulders. "Okay. I hungry."

"You said that." She was hungry too. "Want to share an apple?"

He nodded.

"I'll call when it's ready." She meandered into the kitchen and pulled out a knife and cutting board. Jason didn't like the peel, and she wasn't a fan either. A couple of minutes later she had two plates with sliced apples and peanut butter set out on the bar. "Your apple's ready," she called.

Jason charged into the kitchen. "Yum!" She lifted him onto the stool. "Thanks." He bit into the apple and juice squirted. He giggled. "That was funny." He took another bite and frowned when it didn't happen a second time. "Aiden said we should go to church. What's church, Mommy?"

She frowned. Of course he wouldn't remember going at Easter this past year since he was so young. "It's a place people go to learn about God. We all went together on Easter, but you probably don't remember"

"Oh. Did we sing songs there?"

"Yes."

"I remember. Why do we need to learn about God?"

Her son's constant barrage of questions and demands made her want to climb back into the bubble bath. "God is… who do you think He is?"

"Aiden said He made the world. Did He, Mommy?"

"Yes. I believe He did." She hadn't given creation much thought, but she'd heard enough sermons on Christmas and Easter to get the gist of what Christians believed. Why she hadn't given Him more thought she couldn't say. Her parents didn't attend except twice a year. It was more of a tradition than anything.

"Wow." Awe filled his voice.

"Wow, what?"

"God. He made the whole wide world. That's big, Mommy!"

She grinned. Her son had a flare for the dramatic, but he was right. It was big.

"I want to go to church like Aiden does."

"You realize he doesn't live on the island?"

Her son frowned. "Oh." His face brightened. "Where does Chris go?"

"I guess you will have to ask him when he gets here."

Jason sighed. "I'm finished."

"You may go play now."

He hopped down and charged from the kitchen, flying through the small house like a mini-tornado. At least he didn't leave destruction in his wake.

She quickly wiped the counter down and made sure everything was perfect for when Chris arrived. Her heart beat a little faster in anticipation of his arrival.

CHRIS SETTLED ON THE hillside facing the lake and the movie screen. Jason snuggled between him and Rachel. "It's a good thing you thought to bring several blankets." The thick one they sat on helped keep the cold from his bones.

"When I saw the temperature predicted for this evening I knew blankets were a must. I wouldn't be surprised if we have a dusting of snow before the evening is over."

He looked to the cloud-filled sky. "You may be right."

Jason snuggled against him.

"It's so beautiful here at night," Rachel said.

Chris took in the light display on the grounds of the resort. The shrubs and trees were lit with colored lights, and the pathways with tiny white lights gave off enough illumination to see where one was going, but not so much they wouldn't be able to see the movie once it started.

"I'm glad your plans fell through and you could join us."

Rachel's grin warmed him from the inside out.

"It's nice to have adult company."

"You mean you don't get enough of adults at work?" He preferred working from a home office. Being around a bunch of people all day wore on him. Then again, he was an introvert.

She shook her head. "Not the same."

"I suppose not."

Jason patted his arm. "Can I go church with you?"

He shot a glance toward Rachel. "If your mom says it's okay. Maybe she'd like to join you." The screen lit and sound blasted from the speakers.

"It's starting, Mommy," Jason shouted, their conversation about church suddenly forgotten.

"That's right. Time to be quiet." Rachel held a finger to her lips.

At some point during the movie Jason zonked out. Chris pulled a blanket up to the boy's chin and tucked it around him so no cold air would get to his little body.

"He's been acting off today. He kept saying he's hungry, then would hardly eat. I'm not sure what to think."

"He's probably still learning the difference between hunger and other stomach pains."

"You could be right. I wonder if he's coming down with something." She touched her hand to his cool forehead. "He's pretty cute when he's asleep, huh? Not a care in the world." Rachel whispered.

"That he is. Are you enjoying the movie?" He could take it or leave it and his toes had gone numb.

"It's fine. How about you?"

"Same. You want to go inside and warm up with some hot chocolate before we go on the sleigh ride, or would you rather finish the movie?"

"Going in is a great idea." Relief shone in her eyes. "Would you mind carrying Jason? I'll get the blankets."

"No problem." He stood and scooped the boy up. Jason snuggled into his chest and murmured something about church. Which gave him an idea. He waited for Rachel to gather the blankets, then they strolled side by side into the lobby.

She pointed toward their right. "There's a coffee cart at the end of the hall that serves amazing hot chocolate, much better than that packaged stuff they're giving away outside. How about you find a bench, and I'll get us some?"

He didn't like the idea of her treating, but his hands were otherwise occupied. He nodded and found a quiet, out of the way bench, where Jason wouldn't be disturbed. A short time later, Rachel approached holding two medium-sized cups. "Great spot. I like to come here on my breaks. It's like a secret alcove." She kept her voice low as she sat and handed him his cup.

"Thanks."

"Sure. I'm glad you came tonight."

He chuckled. "We covered that already."

"Oops. When do you move into your house?"

"Can you believe the week of Christmas? That is the worst possible timing on my part. I've had a hard time finding help to move my stuff from storage. I still have a few people left to ask, but I'm beginning to wonder if I should hire someone."

"I'd be happy to help get your stuff moved into your house."

Nick was right, Rachel was nice. "We never finished our conversation about visiting my church. You're more than welcome. I thought you didn't go."

"We don't, but Aiden told Jason he should and now he wants to."

"What about you?" He held his breath praying for the words he wanted to hear.

"I guess I'm a little curious. Zoe invited me to visit her church too. Which I think may be the same place you attend. I might go if Jason pushes the issue."

Way to go Aiden.

"Of course we will attend the Christmas service. That's tradition."

His heart sunk a little. He really wanted Rachel to come to know the Lord, but he also knew pushing wouldn't do any good. "What other traditions do you have?"

"Other than putting up a tree and stockings and baking way too many sweets, none. I'd like for Jason and me to start a few of our own. We've been with my parents his entire life, and we've always done things the way they do. How about you? Any traditions?"

"The usual, like you, and then sometimes I don't do anything. When you live alone it doesn't make a lot of sense to go all out with decorations and whatnots."

"What about your family?"

"My mom moves around to the different houses of friends and family each year. She'll be in New York this year visiting my sister and her family."

"You have a sister?"

He nodded. His family had once been close, but that was before Rick had died. His little brother's death had ripped his once tight family apart. He yawned, covering his mouth. He'd stayed up most of the night working on a project that was due by five this evening. He'd made the deadline, but barely. The laid back atmosphere of island life had seeped into his work habits, and if he wasn't careful, he'd start losing business. His heavy eyelids slid shut. He forced them open.

Rachel looked at him with concern clouding her pretty face. "How about we try this again some other time? You're clearly tired, and it's too cold to enjoy a sleigh ride tonight."

"Are you sure?" He was torn between being excited about leaving and disappointed. But it was freezing outside, and his warm bed sounded nice.

"Yes. I want Jason to be able to enjoy it too and that's not happening tonight."

"If you're sure you don't mind, but I'd still like to do the sleigh ride another time. I've had about two hours of sleep in the last twenty-four."

"Why?"

"Work."

"Is that normal?"

"No, but it's not abnormal either. I do what I have to do to meet a deadline, and since I've been spending so much time not working, I paid the price."

"Then we really should do this another time. I don't want to be the only one awake on the ride."

He chuckled and stood, gathering Jason into his arms. The boy's eyes popped open, and he wrapped an arm around Chris's neck. He could get used to evenings like this. They almost felt like a family. He stilled, unsure at the direction of his thoughts. He couldn't go there—at least not yet.

CHAPTER ELEVEN

Sunday morning Rachel held Jason's hand as they climbed the stairs into the old church building. Her fingers tingled, and her stomach roiled. Why was she so nervous? It was only church, and she'd been invited to be there.

A man held the door open and handed her a program, or something that looked like one. "Welcome."

"Thank you." She stepped inside and warmth enveloped her. It hadn't snowed last night, but it was certainly cold enough. Once December hit, the temperature had dropped dramatically. Even the longtime residents talked about how unusually cold it was this year.

Jason wrenched free from her and tore across the foyer. "Chris!" He launched himself at the startled man.

"Oh no," she moaned as she hustled across to where Jason was now comfortably situated in Chris's arms.

Jason grinned wide and patted the man on the back. "Look, Mommy. Chris is here."

"I see." She wanted to reprimand her son for his behavior but didn't want to draw any more attention than Jason had already done. She wiped her moist hands down the side of her slacks and looked around the small foyer. "Have you seen Zoe? She said she'd be here and invited us to sit with her." Was that a flicker of disappointment in Chris's eyes?

"She and Nick are already seated in the sanctuary." He put Jason down. "Maybe Jason would enjoy the three-and-four-year-olds' class."

Rachel hesitated. Zoe mentioned that there were a few other kids here that were her son's age, and it would be good for him to be around other children. "What do you think, Jason? Would you like to go play with other kids?"

He scrunched his face up and pressed his lips together. She held her breath.

Suddenly his face relaxed, and he shrugged. "Okay." He slipped his hand into hers.

That went much better than expected. Since he spent most, if not all, of his time with adults, she'd been afraid he'd insist on staying with her.

"I'll show you where his class is." Chris led the way down a nearby hall.

After Jason was checked in, they went back to the sanctuary where everyone was standing and singing.

"We're late."

"It's okay. They start like this so latecomers can slip in unnoticed." He grinned. "You're welcome to sit with me, then you won't have to go to the front to be with Nick and Zoe."

That sounded good to her. She trailed him into a nearby row and tried to follow along with the words projected on the screen above the stage, but she'd never heard the song before, so it was tough. She finally decided to simply listen to the blended voices. The result was quite beautiful. Tension melted, and for the first time all morning, she relaxed. Maybe there was something to this church thing after all.

The song ended and everyone sat. After a few more songs, the minister did his thing. The deep, gentle timbre of his voice was easy to listen to. The sanctuary was nicely decorated with holly wreaths on the end of every other row, and red bows on the rows in between. The stage had a life-sized nativity, but was otherwise unadorned. Maybe they held a Christmas pageant. That would be fun for Jason to see. He might even be old enough to remember it.

At the end of the sermon, the preacher asked everyone to stand then prayed a blessing over the people. She turned toward Chris. "That was nice. I've never been in a church where the preacher prayed a blessing like that."

"Pastor Michaels does that every week. I hadn't thought about it, but you're right. Do you have lunch plans?"

"Actually, I do." She'd told Zoe and Nick she'd have lunch with them. "But I'll probably see you, since my plans are at the B&B."

He raised a brow. "Okay. I'm headed to the general store for a sandwich. Do you want help finding Jason's class?"

"I think I can remember. Thanks." She stepped into the aisle and followed the crowd into the foyer.

Someone touched her elbow. She turned and grinned at Chris. "I thought you were leaving."

"I am, but I have a quick question. Will you be coming back next week?"

"We might."

He smiled. "Good. See you." He turned and walked toward the exit.

She found her way to Jason's class and watched him playing with another boy until he noticed her.

"Mommy!" He jumped up and ran to her.

"Hi, buddy. Put the toys away you were playing with, and then we can go."

Her son quickly cleaned up and placed the Mr. Potato Head on a low shelf.

There were two adults in the room—one male, one female. The female handed him some papers. "Don't forget your lesson, Jason. If you memorize the verse and come back next week and tell it to me, you will get to choose from the prize box."

Jason's face lit with excitement.

The male teacher turned to Rachel. "Jason is quite verbal. I would never have guessed he's only three."

"It comes from being around adults all the time. Plus my parents are grammar sticklers and have been working with him since he was old enough to talk. I hope he wasn't a problem."

"Not at all. We enjoyed him."

Rachel held out her hand to him and thanked the teachers before walking away.

"I had fun, Mommy. Can we come back again?"

"We'll see." If the people there found out about her past, they might reject her and her son. One thing was certain, no one could find out about her past, if she decided to go back.

"But I want a prize from the box," he whined.

"I said we'd see." Her firm tone brooked no room for argument. She guided him outside and to the parking lot. "Tell me about what you did."

"We sang songs, played games, listened to a story, colored, had a snack, and at the end we got to play with toys."

She opened the passenger door, and he scrambled inside. After making sure he was secure she got behind the wheel and headed home. Maybe going to church was a good idea. It gave her a break from her mom duties, and she really did enjoy the song time. She didn't exactly recall what the preacher had to say, since her mind wandered most of the time, but Jason seemed to have gotten a lot out of his class.

"Did you know Jesus walked on water?"

"He did? I had no idea. Tell me about it." She glanced at him in the rearview mirror.

"Well there was a storm, and his friends were out on a boat. He walked out to them and told them to not be afraid. Jesus is God's son. Did you know that?"

"Yes. I've heard." She grinned at him through the rearview mirror. "It sounds like you learned a lot today." She wasn't sure what she thought about all of this, but she was open to looking more deeply into Christianity. It wasn't like she didn't believe there was a God, she simply hadn't given Him much thought. Maybe it was time to make a change, at least for Jason's sake.

They went home and dropped off Jason's stuff. She changed into jeans and a sweater then grabbed the fudge from the fridge she'd made to take over to the B&B. "Let's go, Jasie."

"I'm playing," he said from his bedroom.

She found him in the middle of his room building another block tower. "How about you pick out three small toys to take with us and put them in your backpack."

A short time later they pulled into the B&B parking lot. This place felt like a second home, more so than her parents' house.

Her parents were supportive and had given everything to help her and Jason, but she knew they didn't approve of her life choices. They'd made that abundantly clear with thinly veiled hostile remarks. She shook off all thoughts of her parents and unstrapped Jason from his car seat. She waited for him to grab his backpack then they went inside.

"Hello," she called out.

"In the kitchen," Zoe said.

They sauntered into the room. "Mmm. Something smells heavenly."

"Thanks."

"I brought fudge."

Zoe's head whipped toward her, eyes widening. "I love fudge."

"Good." She grinned.

"Have a seat. Lunch won't be ready for a bit. Jason, Nick is downstairs. Would you like to go down and watch a video?"

"Okay."

Rachel followed and quickly settled him on the couch then went back up to the kitchen.

"I saw you sitting with Chris this morning."

"Yes, he showed me where Jason's class was, and by the

time we got into the service, it had started. I didn't want to walk up to where you and Nick were sitting. I hope you don't mind."

A twinkle lit Zoe's eye as she poured them each a cup of coffee. "Not at all. So what did you think?"

"I really enjoyed the singing, and your pastor has a pleasant voice. Jason loved it and begged me to take him back next week." She shrugged and stared into her coffee. "We'll see."

"Why the hesitation?"

Should she tell Zoe how she really felt? Her friend could be trusted and wouldn't judge her, that much she was sure of, but did she want her to know? It wasn't like she was that person anymore. Then again, confession was good for the soul, so maybe talking about it would help. She sat at the island and cradled her coffee cup. She took a bracing breath then met Zoe's curious gaze. "I feel like a fraud when I'm there."

Zoe frowned. "I don't understand. Did someone say something rude to you?"

"No. Everyone was very nice actually." Rachel took a long sip from her cup and set it down slowly. Her mind raced for an appropriate response. "I don't belong there with all of you perfect people. I'm too messed up." Zoe of all people should understand why she felt this way. Her friend knew a little of her past.

Zoe's brow scrunched. "Only one perfect person ever walked on this earth, and it certainly wasn't anyone at any church. Where is this coming from, Rachel?"

CHRIS SAT AT THE dining room table in the B&B eating a club sandwich he'd purchased at the general store. He hadn't meant to eavesdrop, but Zoe and Rachel's voices carried through the quiet house. What did Rachel mean about being too messed up? Other than her spiritual life, she seemed to have it together.

He chuckled softly when Zoe asked her the same question. He could clearly hear Rachel's response "You don't know me all that well, Zoe. Before we met I was wild. My parents said I was sowing my wild oats. I was rebellious and only lived for a good time. Getting pregnant with Jason sobered me up. He changed everything. I suddenly had a choice to make, and I wanted to make the right one. Then when my husband, Jason, died two weeks after we were married, fear put me on the straight and narrow."

She'd named her son after her husband. He half wondered why she hadn't added the junior part, not that it mattered.

Rachel continued. "My son needed a parent, and I didn't want *my* parents raising him because I was too high or drunk to take care of him after a party. I couldn't continue with the lifestyle I'd been living. I'm clean and sober, all the time now, but the things I used to do… let's just say, you don't want to know."

He tuned out Zoe's reply. His appetite dulled. This must be what he sensed Rachel was hiding. The woman Rachel described was nothing like the person he'd gotten to know over the past few weeks. The woman he knew was responsible, caring, put her son before herself. He hadn't seen any drug paraphernalia or an ounce of liquor in her home, nor did he ever smell it on her breath.

Rachel had a past—everyone did, but hers was sketchy at best from the sound of it. He felt torn between anger, denial, and hurt. Not hurt for himself, but for her. He could only imagine the unspeakable… no he wouldn't go there—couldn't. He cared about Rachel as a friend, and as such he would support her, but as a man he wasn't sure he could ignore her past activity. He was angry that she had engaged in that kind of behavior. She was smarter than that.

Then again she had been young and stupid. Lots of young people partied and turned out fine. Clearly Rachel fell into that category. He rested his head in his hands, hurting for her, for them. She'd lost her innocence. Sure she'd been married and had a child, but what she lost was a different kind of innocence, and it grieved him.

He tuned back in to the conversation in the kitchen. "Rachel, I want you to listen to me when I tell you this, because I *know* what I'm talking about. Your past is in the past. My parents lived the life you described, except when they had me, they didn't love me enough to change their ways. I'm proud of you for getting clean and sober. How did you do it? When you were here that summer I saw no sign that you had a substance problem."

"I wasn't an addict or alcoholic, but I knew how to party. It was good that Jason had asked me to come find the ring for him, because it got me away from my old friends and their influence. I was away long enough that they forgot about me, and no one bothered me once I went home to live with my parents. In spite of evidence to the contrary, I'm not a stupid person. I knew what I was doing to myself, and I didn't care, but I could *not* do that to my child, whether I kept him or not."

"That's right. I remember you weren't sure what you were going to do with your baby. Any regrets?"

"Not even one. I love Jason more than anything in the world. I would have hated myself if I'd given him up. Not that adoption is a bad thing, but it would have torn me up inside. Once I realized my parents would support me and help me get on my feet, I knew I would keep him. The money from the ring helped to partially finance culinary school, and my parents gave us a home rent free until I could save up enough to get Jason and me a place of our own."

"I'm proud of you, Rachel, and you shouldn't beat yourself up over your past. The people at church don't need to know how you used to be, and even if they find out, I don't see that they'd have an issue with you. It's no one's business—I happen to know there are people at church who have their own pasts they deal with. I hope you will continue to come to church and learn about the Lord. I have a Bible I'd like to give you. I think the people written about in there will surprise you. They are not only imperfect, but several of them did some pretty rotten stuff, and you know what? God loved them anyway."

Way to go, Zoe. Guilt pressed in on him for eavesdropping. He shouldn't have paid attention to what they were saying, even though he'd been compelled to know why Rachel said she was messed up. He wrapped the remainder of his sandwich and tossed it into the garbage can. He didn't want to be caught sitting here if Rachel left the kitchen.

One thing was certain though, he had some soul searching and praying to do. He'd thought that the only thing between him and Rachel was her not being a Christian, but her past was now an issue as well.

It wasn't fair of him to hold her past against her, but what if she had an STD or what if she relapsed and went back to her old ways? He shook his head, working to shove the thought away. If the Lord should bless him with a relationship with Rachel then it would mean she belonged to Him and she was redeemed.

What she did in her old life wouldn't matter because she would have a new beginning. God would forgive her, and who was he to judge? It wasn't like he was perfect. Sure he'd never felt the desire to party or do the things Rachel had, but he was far from perfect. *What do I do, Lord?*

A peace washed over him. He didn't have to decide now. All he had to do was trust.

RACHEL SNUGGLED INTO THE arm of the couch late Sunday evening with Zoe's Bible cradled in her hands. Zoe had marked several spots she thought she should read. The story about King David mesmerized her. The man was a scoundrel, and his actions did not come without consequences, but God loved him anyway. Astounding. Maybe He could love her, too. But she felt that David was special. Surely God didn't love everyone who messed up like that. She'd have to keep reading to find out, but it was getting late.

A moan from Jason's room drew her attention. Before she tucked him into bed, he'd complained that his tummy hurt. Had it gotten worse? She hurried into his room and placed a hand on his forehead. Worry turned her stomach. His skin was warm to the touch.

CHAPTER TWELVE

CHRIS AWAKENED TO THE SOUND OF his cell phone buzzing. He rolled over and pulled it off the nightstand. "Hello." He cleared his gravelly voice.

"Chris, it's Rachel. I can't get hold of Nick, and there's something wrong with Jason."

He shot out of bed. "What's wrong with Jason?"

"I'm not sure. He has a bad stomachache, and his belly is swollen."

His mind shot to the past. His brother had had similar symptoms and had died from a ruptured appendix. He glanced at the clock—three in the morning. "Does he have a fever?"

"I didn't take it, but he feels hot. Hold on a minute." Her voice wobbled.

His pulse thrummed in his ears. Should he wake Nick or tell Rachel to take her son to the hospital? He didn't want her to have another hospital bill if it turned out to be a stomachache and trapped gas.

"It's one hundred and one."

He ran a hand through the hair at the base of his neck.

"Don't freak out, Rachel, but it sounds like appendicitis to me." He didn't want to tell her about his little brother or she would lose it for sure.

"Will you get Nick please?" She sounded like she was crying.

"On my way." He threw open his door and raced down the stairs. He pounded on Nick's apartment door.

A moment later it opened. Nick stood there looking tousled, but alert. "What's wrong?"

"Rachel needs to talk with you." He thrust his cell phone at Nick and took a step back.

"No. The ferry doesn't run this early. Your only option is Wildflower Hospital. I'll meet you there." He tossed the phone to Chris. "Thanks."

"Do you think it's appendicitis?"

Nick nodded before closing the door.

Now what? He couldn't go back to sleep knowing that Rachel's son was in trouble. He showered and dressed. The walls of his room felt like they were closing in, but going to the hospital right now would be futile. Rachel and Jason would be in an exam room or having tests run. He'd be pacing the hospital waiting room alone.

Lord, please don't let Jason die.

Memories of the day his little brother died flooded his mind—the worst day of his life. If only Rick had said something, maybe they could have gotten him help in time. But his little brother was stoic and had rarely complained about anything, much less not feeling well.

He rubbed the back of his neck and sighed. Pacing the hospital waiting room had to be better than this. As he drove to the hospital it struck him—Rachel's past, though painful, should not and would not come between them. Life and death situations had a way of bringing clarity. He knew without a shadow of doubt that Rachel's past didn't matter to him anymore. She wasn't the person she used to be.

He pulled into the nearly empty parking lot and raced inside, hoping he'd delayed enough to give Nick or whoever time to determine exactly what was wrong with Jason. Who would have thought a three-year-old would spend so much time as an emergency patient? They were all becoming too familiar with the facility.

A vending machine that distributed coffee, tea, and hot chocolate stood near the entrance. He slid in the exact amount of money and purchased a hot chocolate and a coffee, unsure which one Rachel would want, then went to the reception desk. "Excuse me, I'm looking for Rachel and Jason Narrelli." Just then Rachel walked into the waiting room from the direction of the exam area. She looked ready to drop. He rushed to her side. "Coffee or hot chocolate?"

"Coffee. Thanks." She sipped it and made a face. "It's awful."

He gently took the coffee from her hand and gave her the other option. "How's Jason?"

"They did an ultrasound." Her voice hitched. She took a deep breath and let it out slowly. "His appendix hasn't burst, but they must do emergency surgery. They are sedating him and prepping him for surgery."

"They do that kind of thing here on a child?" His brother had been taken to a children's hospital because they needed the right sized equipment.

She nodded. "Apparently, after a child died because they didn't have the proper equipment to treat him, Nick convinced the hospital board that they should be more prepared for young children. The ferry hours make transportation to a pediatric hospital impossible from ten P.M. to six A.M. This place actually has a tiny pediatric wing."

"That's amazing. Nick's foresight might have saved your son's life." He guided her to a set of nearby seats.

She paled. "I hadn't thought about the possibility of him dying." Her hands shook so badly he was afraid she'd drop the cup.

He carefully took the cup from her and placed it on the floor. "Jason is in good hands."

She looked at him with haunted eyes. "He's all I have. What if they don't get to it in time, and his appendix ruptures?"

He draped an arm across her shoulders and pulled her into a hug. "Don't think like that. Many people have survived even a ruptured appendix."

"Right. Positive thoughts—like that will do any good."

He had to agree with her. Positive thoughts wouldn't affect the outcome of the surgery, but one thing would. "May I pray with you for Jason?"

Her eyes teared up, and she nodded. He bowed his head. "Lord, Jason needs Your help. Please guide the surgeon and help him take care of Jason. And Lord, please comfort Jason and give him Your peace. I also ask for Your comfort and peace for his mom. Thanks. Amen." He dropped his arm from her shoulder and sat back. Jason had to be okay. He just had to be. He couldn't die like Rick had.

Chris gazed around the pleasant looking waiting room decorated in earth tones. A huge fish tank with several colorful fish hummed nearby. A fake Christmas tree stood in one corner and garlands with colored lights decorated the reception desk. Funny, he hadn't noticed any of that when he'd first come in. As a rule he hated hospitals, but this one had gone to great lengths to make the place appear pleasant.

Rachel bent and picked up her cup. "Thanks for praying." She sipped the sweet beverage. "May I ask you something?"

"Sure."

"Were you pre-med in college?"

He chuckled. "No. I'm a computer geek through and through. Why do you ask?"

"You knew exactly what was wrong with Jason. How?"

"Oh." He didn't want to go there. She didn't need to hear about Rick, but she deserved an honest answer. "My little brother's appendix burst when he was thirteen. My parents were out of state. They travelled a lot for business. My big sister was eighteen, and they left her in charge. Rick was a tough kid, never one to complain or make a big deal about not feeling well. We had no idea there was anything wrong with him until after it burst." He took a shaky breath. "You sure you want to hear this?"

"Not really, but I think I should."

He sighed. "They operated on him to clean out the bacteria the best they could, but it wasn't enough. Rick fought for his life for a few days, but none of the antibiotics worked. Mom and Dad rushed home. They were devastated, and I could tell they blamed my sister and me. My family was never the same after that."

"No offense, but your parents are stupid. They still had two kids who needed them. There is no way you or your sister should have been blamed."

His head whipped toward her. "They were angry and guilt ridden because they weren't there when Rick needed them. My mom still is sometimes. Dad died a year later from a massive heart attack." He shrugged.

Rachel gasped. "I'm so sorry, Chris. My words were very insensitive."

He took her hand and gave it a squeeze. "They were right to blame us. We were the older siblings and should have noticed something was wrong."

"But you said yourself, he never let on. Plus you were kids yourself. You can't carry that burden."

"But if we were paying attention, we would have noticed that something wasn't right with him."

"Maybe. Maybe not. Jason didn't seem all that sick to me when I tucked him into bed tonight. If I hadn't stayed up late reading I may not have noticed he'd gotten worse until morning. " She rested her other hand over his.

He nodded, unable to find his voice. He'd give about

anything to get that week back and do things differently. He sipped the coffee she said was awful. "You weren't kidding. This stuff is bad. I'm going to get something else. The general store is open by now. Would you like anything?"

She pulled out her wallet and handed him a ten. "Would you get me a large coffee and a bagel with cream cheese?"

"Sure. Keep your money. I've got this."

She shook her head. "Please take it." The look in her eyes said she needed him to take it. She needed to be in control of something, even if it was only paying for her breakfast. He understood that feeling.

"I'll be back soon. Will you be okay?"

She nodded.

He stood and strode toward the sliding doors. Light snow fell, leaving a thin coating on the ground. He groaned. At least it hadn't accumulated yet. He'd be able to get to the store and back with no problem.

RACHEL SAT IN THE waiting room, her stomach in knots. The bagel she asked for would probably go uneaten. Chris's prayer for her son touched her deeply. She admired his strong faith and wished for the same.

After what happened to his brother and then his dad, one would think it would be hard to blindly trust a God who'd allowed such bad things to happen to his family, but who was she to judge? She knew little to nothing about God's ways, and from what she'd read so far, He didn't operate the way she expected.

She'd read a lot about King David the night before, and one thing bugged her. God had caused David's child to die because of what he had done. Would God take Jason because of her past? She didn't want anything to do with Him if He did. She crossed her arms and set her jaw.

I love you—and Jason.

Warmth and peace flowed through her. Where had that thought come from?

"Any word yet?"

She startled and looked up as Chris walked toward her with a cup tray and a sack. She shook her head.

He plopped down beside her. "This coffee smells incredible."

She took the cup he offered and sipped. "That's because it is. Thank you for getting it." She noted snowflakes on his jacket. "It's snowing?" She'd been sitting with her back to the window.

"Yes. It's a winter wonderland out there. But I don't think much more will fall. It appears to be clearing up."

"Good." Fear gripped her. She'd made a lot of mistakes. Would God really make her son pay for her poor choices? "Zoe gave me a Bible yesterday, and I have a question."

"Shoot."

"Will God let my son die because of my mistakes?" Her voice caught in a sob.

CHAPTER THIRTEEN

CHRIS SUCKED IN A SHARP BREATH as he sat beside Rachel in the hospital waiting room. He wrapped an arm around her and rubbed her shoulder. "Absolutely not. What makes you think God would do that?" He hated seeing her so torn up.

She took a deep breath then let it out slowly, clearly trying to compose herself. "He took King David's son because of what he did."

Chris frowned and removed his hand from her shoulder since she'd stopped crying. How did he help Rachel understand that things were different now without getting theological on her? "You said you've gone to church on Christmas and Easter. So you know the Christmas story of Jesus's birth, and you know about His crucifixion and resurrection?"

She nodded. "I haven't decided if it's all true or not though. It's all pretty incredible, but then again it seems that one either accepts all of what the Bible has to say or none of it. So I guess, I'm leaning toward believing it's true, rather than not."

He admired how she processed her thoughts. She was

smart and was taking the time to really think through what she'd read. "Good. And, you believe the part about David is true?"

"Yes."

That she didn't question the validity of the Old Testament, but doubted the truth of the New Testament baffled him. He sent up a quick prayer. *Lord please give me wisdom.*

"It's like this. The Old Testament, which is where the story of David is recorded, falls within the old covenant that God set up with humanity. But when Jesus came as the ultimate sacrifice everything changed."

She shook her head. "I don't understand what you're talking about. I get the part about Jesus being the ultimate sacrifice. According to the sermons I've heard through the years, He was perfect and died on the cross then rose from the dead. His blood was shed to be the ultimate sacrifice for sin."

"Exactly, but in the Old Testament, they had to sacrifice animals. Blood had to be shed to pay for what a person did wrong. They couldn't simply ask for forgiveness. It was much more complicated then."

Her nose wrinkled. "What does this have to do with my question?"

"Long complicated story short—what Jesus did changed how things work and how God deals with people. He is not going to punish Jason because of something you did, especially something you did when you weren't a Christian. David was a believer, and he messed up. God punished him, and then they moved on."

"So if I become a Christian, He will punish me for all the bad stuff I did?"

He shook his head. "When someone asks the Lord into their life then he or she becomes a new person. It's a spiritual re-birth. The old stuff is gone and you start over fresh."

"A clean slate?"

"Exactly."

The puzzled look on her face relaxed. "Thanks for explaining all of that. It's pretty weird, but I think I understand what you're trying to say for the most part. I'm going to take a walk and see if I can find out what's happening with Jason." She stood then turned. "In case I forgot to say it, thanks for being here. I know you have a job and deadlines, so if you need to leave, I understand."

"I'm good. I'll be right here when you get back." He watched her walk over to the reception desk. He tipped his head back and closed his eyes. *Lord, please be with Rachel. I've never talked with anyone like that and even though she said it helped, I feel like I messed it up. And please be with Jason.* The air around him moved, and he felt someone sit beside him. He opened his eyes—Rachel. "What'd you find out?"

"He went in for surgery a little bit ago."

"What took so long?"

"They were waiting for the pediatric surgeon."

The lights in a corner shop flicked on. "Looks like the gift shop is open."

"Good. I want to get something for Jasie." She stood.

He wondered if the nervous energy he sensed had more to do with her spiritual life than Jason's surgery. She knew her son was in good hands, and ever since their talk she hadn't been able to sit still.

RACHEL HAD TO GET away from Chris. His words unsettled her, and she wished he'd leave. All the stuff about an old covenant and sacrifices put her stomach in a knot. As if having her son in surgery wasn't enough! She purchased a coloring book and crayons along with a soft teddy bear with a red bowtie. Rather than head back to sit with Chris, she strolled down an empty corridor.

She knew Chris meant well, and in all fairness she had asked the question, but she wanted to be alone to process everything. A window overlooked a park-like setting. She caught her breath. "How beautiful." She'd been so distracted every time she'd come here, she had no idea there was a gazebo on the hospital grounds or that they had trees decorated with colored lights. Snow fell softly, creating the most beautiful scene. Jason would love this.

Mesmerized, she stared for who knew how long, her mind a jumbled mess. She had so many questions but didn't want to ask Chris. She pulled out her cell phone and called Zoe.

"How's Jason?" Zoe asked without preamble.

"In surgery. I assume it's going well since no one has told me otherwise."

"Good. I want to come over there, but I'm stuck at the B&B on breakfast duty."

"Oh! I'm so sorry. I'll let you go."

"Don't hang up. Things are under control for the moment. How are you holding up?"

"Okay, considering I'm running on almost no sleep. I stayed up until midnight reading the Bible you gave me, then Jason was moaning, and I only was able to doze until he got so loud I thought he needed medical help."

Silence.

"Hello?"

"I'm here. I'm really sorry about Jason, and I'm thinking about the passages I marked for you in the Bible. I'm a little worried about the timing of what you may have read. One of those stories might be freaking you out."

"You knew and you still told me to read it!" How could Zoe have set her up like that?

"Hey, give me a break. I had no way of knowing Jason would need emergency surgery, but I want you to know that God does not work like that anymore. I only marked the passage about David to show you how imperfect he was, but

God loved him anyway."

"I thought the same thing at first, but if He really loved David, why kill his son?"

"I don't have all the answers, and I know it sounds sadistic, but that's the way things were before Jesus. If you keep reading, you'll see that God gave David another son who was a great man."

"I'm really confused, tired, and scared, Zoe." Her voice cracked.

"I'm coming over there. The food has been served. The dishes will keep. Hang tight. I'm on my way."

Rachel burst into tears and put her phone away. She was an absolute mess.

"Rachel?" Chris touched her shoulder. "Hey, what's wrong?" He pulled her into his arms and let her cry.

Her tears gradually slowed, and she rested her head against his chest. His heartbeat, strong and steady, gave her strength. She stepped out of his comforting arms and wiped her eyes with the back of her hand. "Thanks. I'm sorry you saw me lose it."

"I'm glad I was here." He brushed her hair from her face. "Are you okay now?"

She nodded. She wouldn't be okay until she knew her son was, but she would not get emotional again.

"Good, because Nick was looking for you. The surgery went fine."

Her heart leapt. "Where's Nick?"

"Right here." He stood at the end of the corridor and walked toward them. "I saw Chris come this way and figured that you'd be here. I told Doctor Howard, the pediatric surgeon, I'd fill you in. Jason is fine. He's in recovery. A nurse will take you to him as soon as he wakes up."

The tears started again. She laughed and cried. "Sorry. I don't think my body knows how to respond."

Nick patted her shoulder. "You're tired and stressed. Being emotional is normal."

"Thanks." Her baby was okay. She needed to be with him. "How long until he wakes?"

"It shouldn't be long. Your son is a trooper. I'll check in on him later today. For now, it's time for my rounds." Nick went back in the direction he'd come.

"Do you want me to stay?" Concern filled Chris's kind eyes.

"Zoe is on her way. Thanks for being here with me, Chris." She wrapped her arms around his middle and rested her head against his chest. She liked the feel of his arms around her. She hugged him a little longer than normal before stepping back. "You're a good friend."

"Call if you need anything." He placed a soft kiss on her forehead.

Her stomach fluttered. She looked into his face, knowing without a doubt she cared deeply for this man even if she didn't understand everything he said. "I will. Drive safe. The snow is really starting to accumulate."

He frowned as he looked toward the window and the winter wonderland. "At least I don't have far to go." With one last fleeting look toward the window, he turned and walked away.

Taking a bracing breath, she squared her shoulders and returned to the waiting room. A man sat alone in one corner, and a couple with several children stood at the reception desk. The place had come to life in the short time she'd stepped away.

"Mrs. Narrelli," A nurse wearing teal-colored scrubs called.

Rachel waved and walked toward her, lugging along her gift store purchase. "How's Jason doing?"

"He woke up and is asking for you. If you'll come this way I'll take you to him."

Rachel followed her through a series of corridors until they came to a door marked *Recovery*. Her heart pounded. No matter what, she must stay calm and not upset Jason.

"Your son will be a little loopy, so don't be alarmed."

"Okay. Thanks for the warning."

The nurse opened the door. "He's behind the first curtain on the right." She scooted the curtain back.

"Hi, Jasie." Rachel moved to his side and rested her hand on his forehead.

"Hi, Mommy. Tiger's wike wollipips."

Rachel grinned. The nurse wasn't kidding about him being loopy. "I like lollipops too."

He mumbled something indecipherable.

An orderly walked into the small, curtained-off space. "I'll be taking him up to a room now." He fiddled with a few gadgets, converting the bed into a rolling gurney. "How are you doing, Jason?"

"You big."

The man chuckled. "I get that a lot."

Rachel would have reprimanded her son, but it was pretty cute hearing him talk uncensored and more like a kid his own age. She kind of missed the baby talk that had disappeared for the most part about three months ago.

She walked on the other side of the gurney, and they rode an elevator up to the third floor. Within ten minutes, Jason was settled and sound asleep. She hadn't even been able to give him his gifts. A light knock on his door drew her attention.

Zoe poked her head inside. "May I come in?"

Rachel stood and hugged her friend. "Thanks for coming."

"That's what friends are for, and in case I forgot to mention it earlier, you are not to come to work until Jason is out of here."

"Thanks. I should run home to pick up a few things, but I plan to spend the night as long as he is here."

"Good idea. Since he's still out of it would you like to go now, or I could bring some stuff by later for you?"

"I might slip out, but first I want to ask you a question."

"Shoot." Zoe pulled up another chair and sat.

"Do you think God is punishing me for my mistakes?"

Zoe's eyes lit like fire. "Absolutely not. I tried to explain that over the phone, but I guess I wasn't clear." She suddenly looked nervous. "Please don't be offended by this, but you are not His... yet. He's a forgiving God, Rachel. But until you come to a place where you are ready to commit to Him, He doesn't expect anything from you. Have you read any of the pages I bookmarked toward the end of the Bible?"

Rachel shook her head.

"Read those and then what I'm saying will make more sense. Clearly you believe in God."

"I do, but I don't know what to do about it—or if I even *want* to do anything."

"That's okay. Read the Bible. I'll answer your questions the best that I can."

"Thanks." She looked to her son. He slept peacefully. "You'll sit with him until I get back?"

Zoe pulled a culinary magazine from her oversized purse. "I brought something to read. Take your time."

Rachel nodded, but she would hurry nonetheless. She did not want Jason waking up while she was gone.

She charged into a waiting elevator and rushed out as soon as the door opened. People milled about, a child cried uncontrollably in her mother's arms. The hospital was a flurry of activity. Even the gift shop had a line. She'd left her gift for Jason in his room. The glass doors slid open, and she stepped into the snow-covered parking lot.

"Brr." She hadn't thought to grab a coat in her rush to get here in the wee hours of the morning. Her boots made fresh prints in the snow, which looked to be about an inch deep as she hurried to her Subaru.

She started the engine then hit the wipers and then defrost. It would take a while before she could leave. She willed the process to go faster. Funny, it seemed she was always rushing. Slowing down sounded nice, but there was no time to take life at an easy pace. There were so many demands on her, from caring for her son, to working, to figuring out what was going on in her head about God and her feelings for Chris.

With the windows now clear, she set out for home. She still couldn't believe Chris had come to the hospital. She felt bad about waking him and then avoiding him when he came to keep her company. Even though he didn't seem to mind, she owed him an apology, which he would get as soon as she had a moment to herself.

Her tires slipped a little as she rounded a corner. Her stomach tightened—her car was all-wheel drive. It must really be slick. She kept going, unwilling to stop and get stuck like the Prius she'd just passed on the side of the road. *A Prius?* It couldn't be. She slowed and checked her mirror—Chris. She pulled to the side and ran back a hundred feet to the car. Sure enough, Chris sat inside. She knocked on the window.

He opened the door.

"You want a ride?"

"How about a tow? I have rope in back."

She looked at his tires and shook her head. "You need new tires. You're not going anywhere in that car. Come on, I'll give you a lift to the B&B, and you can call a tow truck."

He frowned, but didn't argue as he got out and locked up. "Where were you heading? I'm surprised to see you here."

"I was running home to shower and pack a bag for myself and Jason. I thought he'd like to have a few of his books. I'm going to be staying in his room at the hospital until he's released." She slipped into her vehicle and waited for Chris to buckle up before pulling out. The tires spun once, she eased off the gas a little, and they moved forward. "I'm sorry that you got stuck, but I'm glad I saw you. I wanted to apologize for waking you this morning and to thank you for sitting with me. I'm sorry I wasn't better company. When I'm stressed or overemotional, I prefer to be alone."

"No apology necessary. I understand, and I'm glad you called. It makes me feel good that you were comfortable enough to call me in the middle of the night."

She glanced at him then quickly returned her gaze to the

road, which was getting worse by the minute. Her windshield wipers flapped back and forth in double time. "It's snowing harder. I thought this island didn't get weather like this." She frowned. Maybe leaving the hospital was a bad idea. No, it would be fine. Her car had gone over the snow-covered Stephens and Snohomish Passes numerous times with little problem.

"I hope I can find a tow truck on this island."

"You will. There's a mechanic not far from downtown."

He chuckled.

"What?"

"The idea of anyplace in Wildflower being called downtown is a stretch of the imagination."

She grinned. He was right, but businesses had popped up all around the general store, which had rapidly become downtown Wildflower. "Will you be okay at the B&B without a car or any means to feed yourself?" She pulled into the driveway.

"I'll be fine. It's not like Nick and Zoe will neglect the B&B, but there's always the manager, Jill. She's extremely helpful."

"I forget about her. I'm not used to dealing with anyone but Zoe and Nick." She stopped as close to the front door as she could. "Here you go. Thanks again."

"Thank *you*! Who knows how long I would have frozen sitting in my car if you hadn't come along. Where are all the tourists when you need one?"

She laughed. "I'll call you and let you know how Jason is doing."

"Okay. Bye." He hesitated, and before she realized what was happening, he kissed her cheek. "Drive safe." He slid out.

She touched the warm spot his lips had left on her skin. Now that was unexpected. Did it mean what she hoped? Did Chris have feelings for her?

CHAPTER FOURTEEN

CHRIS STEPPED INTO WILDFLOWER hospital and detoured to the gift shop. He hadn't seen or spoken with Rachel since yesterday when he'd impulsively kissed her cheek. Maybe it was lack of sleep or simple gratitude for being rescued, he didn't know, but what he did know was that he needed to see her again—and the little guy. He had to see with his own two eyes that Jason was okay.

"Good afternoon, sir. May I help you find something?" The woman working behind the counter asked.

"I would like to take a three-year-old patient a gift. Any ideas?"

"How about a deck of Go Fish cards?"

"Great idea." He took the box she held out to him, then spotted a pretty Christmas floral arrangement with red and white carnations, along with greenery and shiny Christmas bulbs in red, gold, and silver and brought it to the counter as well.

"I don't think a three-year-old will appreciate flowers." She grinned. "Not that I don't want the sale."

He chuckled and pulled out his wallet. "The flowers are

for his mom."

A twinkle lit her eyes. "Lucky lady."

He would never call Rachel lucky, but she was a special lady, who he couldn't get off his mind. "Thanks." Bypassing the elevator, he climbed the stairs to the third floor. His fitness had suffered since coming to the island, and he needed to get in mini-workouts wherever possible.

As he pulled open the door to the pediatric wing, he took a few deep breaths. He was more out of shape than he'd realized. The nurse's station was situated a few feet ahead. He strolled up to a woman on duty. "Hi there, I'm here to see Jason Narrelli."

She smiled warmly. The floor was very quiet as if Jason might be the only patient in the department. "Jason is a cutie. He and his mom are in the first room on the right."

"Thanks." He nodded and strode to the nearby room. The door hung open. "Hello," he said quietly as he entered the room. Jason lay sleeping, cuddling a soft looking, chocolate-colored teddy bear, and Rachel sat reading a Bible.

She looked up and smiled. "You came." Her eyes widened when she spotted the flowers.

He held the arrangement out to her. "For you. I thought it might cheer up his room and help you remember that Christmas is only two weeks away."

She stood and took the bouquet. "It's beautiful. No one has ever given me a Christmas arrangement. Thank you." She set the flowers on the windowsill where sunlight glinted off one of the baubles.

"I brought Go Fish for Jason."

"He'll love it. He's been sleeping a lot. The nurse said that's normal. But once he starts to feel better you can be sure he will enjoy playing. Can you sit and visit or do you need to leave?"

"I can stay for a bit." He carried in a padded, vinyl-covered chair near to Rachel so they could talk quietly and not wake her son. "How are you doing?"

"I'm okay. Jason slept soundly all night, so I was able to doze. Although this chair converts to a bed, it's not the most comfortable. Did you already get your car taken care of?"

"Yes. The mechanic you mentioned had time yesterday. Have you had a chance to go outside and enjoy the snow?"

"No. I hope it sticks around long enough for Jason to appreciate it. He was really looking forward to experiencing snow for the first time."

"As cold as it is, I doubt that it will melt soon." Speaking of melting, he was roasting. He shrugged out of his coat. "I take possession of my house this Friday, and I'll be painting all weekend. I want the walls finished before the flooring guys get there Monday morning. They promised to have the flooring finished in both the apartment and the house by the end of the day on Tuesday. I'd like to re-do some fixtures, but that will keep until later."

"Wow, that's a lot. Plus, you're getting in a week early. How did that happen?"

"I'm guessing since I paid cash things moved faster. I finally found a few friends to help empty my storage unit on Saturday, but I'm considering hiring a company to bring everything over on Wednesday instead. I'm anxious to get into my own place. Don't get me wrong, the B&B is great, but there's nothing like sleeping in your own bed."

"Agreed, but good luck finding anyone this close to Christmas."

He shrugged. "If I can't, then I'll stick with my original plan."

"Jason should be back to normal or at least close by then. If you need help, let me know."

With all she was dealing with, he couldn't believe she'd even consider helping. Surely she needed a break. But he liked spending time with her. "I won't turn down the help. Thanks. Is there anything I can do for you while you're here?"

She started to shake her head, then a sheepish look settled

on her face. "Actually I have a huge favor to ask. Let's talk in the hall."

His curiosity piqued, he stood and led the way.

Rachel closed the door and kept her voice low. "Jason and I were going to get a tree yesterday. Now I don't see being able to do that at all. Do you think you could help me out and set up a small tree in our living room? I'll pay of course," she quickly added.

"I'd be happy to do that for you. You said small. Define small?"

"No more than six feet and not too fat. Smaller is fine. I don't want it to take up the whole room. I don't have a tree stand, so you'll need to get one of those too."

"You've never had a tree before?"

"I've always been at my parents'."

He'd forgotten Rachel's history and how much younger Rachel was than him, which amazed him considering how upset he'd been to learn about her sowing wild oats, as she said her parents said. "Don't worry. I'll find the perfect tree. What about decorations?"

"We planned to make them, but I'm afraid he's not going to feel up to it now."

"I'll figure something out. Are you picky?"

She shrugged. "I don't think so."

"Good." He had an idea, but if she was picky it wouldn't work.

"I'll get you my house key before you leave."

"If it's okay with you, I'd like to get started on finding a tree right away."

"Okay. Be right back." She slipped into her son's room and returned a moment later with her purse. "Here's my key." She dug out her wallet, and he couldn't help but notice it was empty of cash. She quickly flipped to her checkbook.

"Don't worry about the cost, Rachel. This is my gift to you." Missing work so much had probably taken a toll on her finances.

"But you gave me that beautiful flower arrangement."

He grinned. "So, maybe I enjoy giving. Don't spoil my fun."

She tucked her wallet away. "Thank you. Again."

"My pleasure. Now you take good care of yourself and that boy."

She looked ready to cry.

"Come here." He tugged her close. "Everything is going to be okay." He pressed a kiss to the top of her head. "Sometimes life can seem pretty unfair and downright rotten, but you and Jason are going to be okay. You have family and friends who care about and love you." He leaned back slightly and tipped her chin up. "I'm here for you, Rachel. Whatever you need."

"Why? We've only known each other for a short time."

"Some friendships are like that." He wanted to be so much more than her friend but held back. She wasn't ready. And with the circumstances the way they were, neither was he.

RACHEL STOOD STARING OUT the window in Jason's hospital room. The grounds were truly lovely covered in snow. She hoped Chris had good tires now and wouldn't slide off the road again. Especially since she'd sent him on a mission—she'd feel horrible if he had any car troubles because of her.

"Mommy," Jason croaked.

She whirled around. "Hey, buddy. It's about time you woke up. How are you feeling?"

"Okay. I'm hungry."

She chuckled. "I'm glad." She pressed the button for the nurse. "Chris came by this afternoon. He brought you a present."

Jason's eyes widened. "What?"

She handed him the deck of Go Fish cards.

"Cool!"

She pressed her lips together to keep from laughing at his enthusiastic exclamation.

The nurse came into the room her eyes going directly to Jason, then to Rachel.

"Jason is hungry. Is it too late for him to have dinner?"

"Let me check." She slipped from the room and returned about fifteen minutes later with a small bottle of apple juice. "The doctor said liquids are fine for now. He will be in soon to check on Jason."

"Okay. Thanks."

Jason drank about half the juice. "That's yummy, Mommy. I want that at our house."

"You think so, huh?"

An hour later a knock sounded on the door, then it swung open and Nick walked in. "How's my favorite patient?" He looked to Rachel and lowered his voice. "I hope you don't mind if I check on Jason rather than Doctor Howard. I volunteered to keep an eye on him."

"It's better this way, since he knows you."

"That's what I thought too."

"I like apple juice." Jason grinned.

"Glad to hear it. May I listen to your tummy talk?"

"My tummy doesn't talk." He giggled then gasped, his face twisted. "That hurt."

"That's normal, but try not to laugh." He applied the stethoscope to various spots on Jason then stood up. "Everything sounds good." He examined the surgical area next. "Have you tried walking yet?"

Jason shook his head.

"How about you and your mom take a walk and see how far you can get?"

"Okay." Jason looked to her for approval.

"That sounds like a good idea. Would you like to go now?"

"Yes."

"That a boy." Nick helped him from the bed and attached the IV bag to a rolling pole. "It might be painful to walk, but I want you to go as far as you can."

Jason made a face as he stepped toward the door. "I don't want to walk, Mommy."

"How about you go to the door and back," Nick said. "Then I'll help you get back in bed."

Rachel held her breath, unsure what her son would do.

Jason's little face scrunched up. "Okay." One slow step at a time, he made it to the door and the four or so feet back to the bed.

"Way to go." Nick patted him on the back and gently placed him back on the bed. "I think that calls for a Popsicle reward."

Jason grinned. "I like banana."

"One banana Popsicle coming up. I'll send Nurse Stacy in with it soon." He motioned for Rachel to follow him into the hall. "If he continues to progress so well, I expect to release him tomorrow."

"Okay. So everything is fine?"

"His incision site looks great and everything appears normal." He squeezed her shoulder. "Don't worry, Rachel. Your son is healing nicely. I'll be by tomorrow."

"Thanks." She stepped into the room. For the first time in days she truly felt like everything was going to be okay.

"Can we play Go Fish?"

"Sure." She opened the box and slid out the cards.

"Did I hear someone ask about Go Fish?"

Chris's voice sent a tingle zipping through Rachel. She turned and saw him standing in the doorway. "This is an unexpected surprise. What are you doing back?"

"I took care of what you asked, at least mostly, and was hoping to get in a few hands of Go Fish."

"Yay!" Jason finally had the brace off his arm and clapped his hands. His face sobered. "But no laughing. It hurts."

Chris shot her a questioning look.

"When he laughs it pulls on his incision site."

"Oh."

Rachel shuffled then dealt the cards. She couldn't believe Chris came back. Her insides warmed at the kindness of this man. He had the true Christmas spirit. Or was there more than Christmas spirit at play? When she thought about her friends here on the island they were different from the people she knew at home. Not that her friends were horrible people, but they were missing the spark she saw in Zoe, Nick, and Chris.

Chris caught her eye as he held out his hand of cards to Jason. She had the sudden image of the three of them as a family, and it was lovely. A warm-to-your-toes kind of feeling. Did Chris see the same thing? Her face warmed as his eyes questioned her as if he could read her mind. She shook off the thoughts and focused on the game.

Chris took out his phone and held a finger to his lips. "I know phones are frowned on, but we could use Christmas music." He swiped the screen, and a few seconds later, *Oh Holy Night* played and peace filled the room.

Rachel hummed along to the familiar song. She loved Christmas music. The game ended quickly, and Jason's eyes drooped.

"I should go." Chris stood.

"Would you like to take a walk on the grounds? Someone did a beautiful job decorating the trees outside. I'd love to take a walk and stretch my legs."

"What about Jason?" He nodded toward her son.

"The nursing staff is here and have my cell phone number, plus he can barely keep his eyes open. He'll be sound asleep any minute."

He grinned and shrugged into his jacket. "In that case, I'd love to walk in the freezing cold with you."

She grabbed her purse, knit hat, gloves, and coat, kissed Jason goodnight, and closed the door behind them. On the way to the elevator, she told the nurse where she'd be and reminded her to call if Jason needed her.

As the elevator carried them to the main level she donned her winter wear. "Thanks for walking with me. I had to escape that room, and I've wanted to check out the gardens here since the night of Jason's surgery. There's a place with a gazebo that looks so inviting." The doors slid open, and they strolled arm in arm into the night.

Snowflakes cascaded in soft puffs, creating a hush in the night. The snow creaked as it compacted under their feet. She breathed in deeply. "I love the smell of snow."

He chuckled. "I can't smell it."

"Not everyone can."

"Describe it to me."

"Clean. Fresh. It's difficult to explain."

He chuckled. "I think I can smell it after all."

The sidewalk had been cleared, and they strolled around the building until they came to a sign that welcomed them to Reflection Park. "I didn't realize this was a park. I thought it was part of the hospital," Rachel said as they entered the park-like setting she'd viewed from the window. She stopped to soak in the sight. "Isn't it beautiful?"

He slipped his arm from her hold and instead draped it across her shoulder and pulled her close. "Yes. Very. I've never appreciated the lights of Christmas as much as I have since being on Wildflower Island."

She gazed at the colored lights on the huge fir tree. "We should take a selfie with the tree."

"I'm game if you are." A snowflake landed on his cheek and quickly melted.

They plodded across the snow to the tree. She pulled off a glove then grabbed her phone from her pocket and held it up. "Say Merry Christmas on three. One, two."

"Merry Christmas," they said in unison as she snapped the shot. She held the phone out for Chris to see. "What do you think?"

"Nice. Let me get one of you."

She placed a hand on her hip and turned sideways posing like a movie star and grinning as he chuckled. "Okay, your turn." He took her place, and she clicked off a few pictures.

"Will you send me the one of us and the one of you?" She would print and frame them for her dresser to always remember this night.

"Sure, but not until I get the feeling back in my fingers. Let's go check out the gazebo." She skipped like a child through the snow. The worries of her life melted for the moment. "This reminds me of that scene in the *Sound of Music* where Liesl leaps from the benches singing." She stepped onto the bench, rested a hand on Chris's shoulder, and hummed the tune.

"Next thing I know, you'll be running in circles dancing and singing at the top of your lungs," he teased.

She shook her head, laughing. "I'm much too old to behave in such a silly way."

"Until your body stops working, you're not too old."

"In that case..." She sang the chorus and leaped off the bench. She grasped his hands. "Waltz with me."

"You're a nut." He laughed, then hummed along, indulging her.

She giggled like a child as they whirled around the gazebo. Dizziness gripped her, stopping her feet.

Chris stopped with her, but kept his hold on her and drew her even closer. "That was the most fun I've had since... I don't know when. Thank you." He tilted his head and kissed her.

His lips, soft as butter, warmed her from head to toe. She kissed him back. Turning her head and resting it against his chest, she sighed with contentment. She could stay like this forever, but Jason was upstairs and reality awaited. She tilted her head back and met his gaze. "That was fun."

He gave her a quick peck. "I agree. But I should head home. This day has suddenly caught up to me."

"I understand." She felt the effects of the past few days too after having a moment of release and relaxation. Her body craved a good night's sleep in her own bed, but she would stay in that chair one more night.

At the hospital doors, he drew her close once more. "I'm praying for you, Rachel. I hope that's okay."

"Of course."

He grinned. "'Night."

She watched him trudge off into the parking lot and wished tonight could have gone on forever. But reality awaited. Her cell phone rang. She dug in her purse for it. Where was it? Finally! Caller ID listed the hospital, then it stopped ringing. Panic gripped her as she ran inside.

CHAPTER FIFTEEN

RACHEL WILLED THE ELEVATOR TO MOVE faster. Why was the thing moving so stinking slow? "Come on." She pressed the third floor button repeatedly. Why wouldn't this thing move any faster? Tears clogged her throat. She never should have left Jason alone.

The doors finally slid open. She bolted out and rushed to her son's room. "Ja—" She clamped her lips together at the sight of her son sleeping soundly. What was going on? She turned and marched to the nurses' station. "Why did the hospital call me? I couldn't get to my phone fast enough. I thought there was an emergency with my son." Her voice caught.

The nurse gave her a sympathetic look. "I don't know why you received a call, but I do know it wasn't from anyone in this department. I haven't left this spot since you went for a walk, and all the phones are at my station. Did the person leave a message?"

Rachel's cheeks warmed. She slipped her hat from her head. "I didn't think of that. I panicked when I saw it was the hospital. Sorry." She pulled out her phone and listened to the message, then explained to the nurse. "It was Doctor Jackson. Everything is fine. I'm really sorry for freaking out on you."

"No worries. Having a child in the hospital is high stress. It happens to the best. You are doing fine, Rachel."

"Thanks." Totally embarrassed, she went into her son's room. Nick had called to invite them to their place on Christmas Eve for dinner and a Christmas carol sing-along. She'd RSVP later after she calmed down and caught her breath.

She converted the chair into a bed. Making herself as comfortable as possible she pulled out the Bible again and began reading the passages Zoe had marked toward the back. She'd noticed the book was divided into Old Testament and New Testament like Chris had said and decided she liked the new one better. The message of hope drew her.

She read all the book of John before her eyes grew too heavy to continue any further. She was beginning to understand what Zoe and Chris had tried to tell her. Jesus doing what He did changed everything. Awed at His selfless act, she closed her eyes. *I'm beginning to understand what You did for me. It's hard to believe anyone would voluntarily go through the kind of torture You suffered for someone like me, or anyone for that matter, but I get it. Thank You.*

She rolled over, contemplating the words she'd read and how they related to her life. She wanted the kind of peace she saw in her friends' eyes. How did she get it?

CHRIS SAT AT THE table in his room at the B&B clicking away on his laptop. He couldn't keep the grin off his face. The time spent with Rachel had been a much needed break from work. All in all, the day had been one of the best he could remember. From delivering and setting up a tree in Rachel's living room, to playing Go Fish with her son, to waltzing in the gazebo. He'd gone shopping at a thrift shop for the ornaments, but didn't hang them, convinced Rachel and her son would want to do the honors.

His only regret of the day—the kiss. Caught up in the moment, he'd let his feelings trounce good judgment. He couldn't let that happen again, and he knew he'd be very tempted since he'd enjoyed kissing her so much. He cared for her, but unless he could commit his heart, he had no business kissing her like that.

He shook away the thoughts of Rachel. It was time to focus on the screen in front of him. These late nights were going to catch up to him, but for now they were worth it.

A knock sounded on his door. He stood and opened it. "Nick. Is everything okay?"

"Yes. I saw the light under the door when I was doing a walk-through and wanted to invite you to dinner on Christmas Eve. We are inviting the staff and several friends for food and Christmas carols."

"That sounds like fun." Plus he had nothing else planned. "I'd love to come. Thanks for inviting me. Will anyone else I know be there?"

Nick grinned. "As a matter of fact, I invited a certain lady and her son, as well as Piper and Chase, Jill, and a few others you may or may not have met."

"Count me in." He'd only briefly met the resort owners, Piper and Chase, but they seemed like good people. He hadn't realized they were close with Nick and Zoe, but now that he thought about it, Zoe worked for them, so it made sense.

This was turning out to be one of the best Christmases he could recall, at least as an adult. His cell rang. He raised a brow when he read the caller ID and snagged it off the desk. He quickly answered. "Rachel? Hey there, everything okay?"

"Can't sleep. I was taking a chance you might still be up since you're a night owl."

"I am." He sat on the bed and crossed his legs at the ankles.

"Why can't you sleep?" He could think of several reasons she'd still be awake, the uncomfortable sleeping quarters at the top of his list.

"I was reading the Bible again. And I have a question, if you don't mind." Her words tumbled out. "I planned to call Zoe, but I know how tired she is this time of night and well…"

"Relax, Rachel. I'm glad you phoned. What's your question?" He only hoped he wouldn't botch this up like he'd done the last time she had a question about the Bible.

"That's the tough part. I'm not really sure how to word it, but I'll do my best. The thing is, after reading the book of John I realized I don't want what Jesus did to be for nothing, at least where I'm concerned. I read that He died for everyone and all I have to do is receive Him, but I don't know how. Does that make sense?"

He grinned so wide his cheeks hurt. "Perfect sense. I wish we could do this in person, but visiting hours are over."

"The phone is fine. I really want to have what you, Zoe, and Nick have."

"Confess your sins to the Lord and believe in your heart that Jesus was raised from the dead, and you are saved."

"That's it. That's all I have to do to have the peace I see in all of you?"

"Pretty much. I suggest you keep reading the Bible and asking questions." Silence met his ears. "Are you still there?"

"I am. But I realized I've done a *lot* of stuff I need to confess."

He chuckled. "Maybe you should be more general. I don't think He expects you to remember everything you've ever done wrong."

"Oh, good idea." Relief filled her voice. "Thanks, Chris. I'm going to go now."

"Good night, Rachel. Thanks for trusting me with something so important." He laid the phone beside him and hopped off the bed. Suddenly revived, he went back to his computer. A light pain in his arm and chest gripped him and shot fear through him.

RACHEL HAD CHANGED INTO sweats to sleep in, but sleep would not come. As tired as she was she needed to do something about what Chris had told her—now. She rolled off the chair, slipped shoes and a sweater on, then went in search of the little chapel she'd been told was someplace on this level.

At the end of the hall, her search was rewarded. She stepped into the small, darkened room, lit only with a dim light over the front. She walked forward, passing three small benches, and sat on the front row. Soft music played, which she hadn't noticed at first. Closing her eyes, she soaked in the familiar hymn. Even though she hadn't grown up in church, *Amazing Grace* was one of the few hymns she knew and loved.

Lord, I want Your amazing grace to save me, too. I am sorry for all the things I've done wrong. I believe in You and want You to be part of my life. Please give me the same peace I see in my new friends. Thanks.

She sat and listened as the hymn continued to play. Moved by the music or perhaps her newfound faith, tears streamed down her face, and she didn't even care. The peace she'd longed for cradled her. She cried harder as the guilt from her past melted away. She felt free from the burden she'd carried for the past four years. She looked up, knowing without a doubt she'd made the best decision of her life.

A tissue box at the end of the bench caught her eye. It looked like she wasn't the only one who became emotional in this room. She tugged a few tissues from the box and wiped her face. She had no idea how long she'd sat there, but the desire to sleep finally hit her. She headed back to her son's room, knowing that for the first time in a long time, she'd sleep peacefully—even though someone would be in to check on Jason every now and then.

Christmas now meant more to her than ever, and she couldn't wait to celebrate.

CHAPTER SIXTEEN

THE FOLLOWING MORNING, RACHEL PULLED INTO her driveway and grinned when she spotted Chris walking out her front door. She'd hoped he'd received her message, that he still had her house key. Nick was so impressed by Jason's progress he'd released him at nine this morning with the promise that she would call if Jason showed any sign of trouble. "We're home, Jasie."

"Okay. I still want to play in the snow." His bottom lip stuck out, and he sat with crossed arms.

They'd been having this conversation ever since he first spotted the snow in the hospital parking lot. "I know. Maybe we can work on a snowman tomorrow. Let's give your body one more day to heal." She got out and was immediately pulled into Chris's arms. "Well, hello." This wasn't like Chris, but she'd roll with it.

"Welcome home." His lips found hers.

Her insides jolted in unexpected pleasure. "Wow. What was that for?"

"I'm happy you're here."

She laughed. "Me too. Will you carry Jason in for me? I

forgot he didn't have shoes on when I took him to the hospital."

"My pleasure. I hope you don't mind that I went inside your house. I got here early, and it was freezing in my car. I turned your heater up a bit. It was pretty cold in there too."

"I don't mind at all. And thanks for turning the heat up."

"Sure." He opened the back door and unstrapped her son. "How you doing, little dude?"

"I want to play in the snow."

"I see." He scooped him into his arms. "That might be uncomfortable with your stitches."

Jason let out a puff of air in exasperation.

Rachel covered her mouth so he wouldn't see her smile. That would only frustrate her son even more. She grabbed her bag and followed Chris and Jason. Inside, warm air and the scent of pine enveloped her. The tree stood undecorated except for lights in the front window. "You couldn't find any ornaments?"

Disappointment washed over her. She'd thought for sure Chris said he'd taken care of everything, but now that she thought about it, he'd said mostly. It was fine. She could decorate it, and Jason would probably enjoy helping too.

"I like the Christmas tree, Mommy."

"Good." She raised a brow as she faced Chris.

"The box under the tree has ornaments. I knew how much Jason wanted to do it, so I skipped that part."

A surge of affection for this man replaced the disappointment and almost overwhelmed her. His thoughtfulness, his kind heart… everything about him drew her to him. But did he feel the same way toward her?

"Can we decorate it now?" Jason asked.

"I don't see why not. Would you like to stay and help, Chris?"

"I'd like that a whole lot more than what I have to do. But I have an appointment on the mainland. Your keys are on the kitchen counter." He mussed up Jason's hair. "Goodbye, buddy." A shadow crossed his face.

"'Bye." Jason walked gingerly to the tree. "Come on, Mommy."

She glanced down at her son then up at Chris. Something wasn't right with him. He looked worried—uneasy. Why? Since she'd met him he'd been easygoing and upbeat. What could possibly be bothering him?

She wanted to question him, but if he wanted to tell her, he would. She needed to respect his privacy. After all, she hadn't told him every little thing about herself. "Thanks for everything, Chris." She took his hand and gave it a squeeze. "Will you call me later?"

"I'll try." He left without a backward glance.

Why did she feel as though he'd just walked out of their lives for good? But if that's the case, why did he greet her like that? She shook off the thought. Of course he would be back. They were at the very least friends, and she hoped on their way to being much more, especially in light of the kiss he'd greeted her with.

She pushed her concern to the back of her mind and plastered on a smile for Jason while she pried the lid off the fancy box that held compartments for each ornament. These weren't cheap drugstore baubles. Well, maybe a few were, but most weren't. She pulled a delicate glass ball in shades of purple, blue and green from the box and held it to the light. It was iridescent. "It's so beautiful." *And very breakable.* Where had these come from?

"I hang it." Jason reached for the ball.

"Mommy will do this one." She handed him what looked to be a candy cane made from clay. The kind she used to make at school and they'd bake in the oven then paint. Whose ornaments were these? Surely they weren't Chris's.

She wondered at the man's demeanor. She should stop thinking about him, but worry knotted the pit of her stomach as she reached for another clay-like ornament and handed it to

Jason. If Chris wanted her to know his personal affairs he'd tell her. She needed to think about something else. Like baking Christmas cookies to take to Zoe and Nick's on Christmas Eve. There couldn't be too many cookies to her way of thinking. Maybe she'd bake a couple of pies while she was at it.

It was nice that Nick and Zoe were closing the B&B from Christmas Eve to New Years to allow their staff to spend time with family and friends. Her mind drifted back to Chris again. Did he have plans for Christmas?

CHRIS SAT ON THE exam table in his doctor's office. His chest ached for lack of a better word. He knew in his gut this wasn't simply anxiety. Something was seriously wrong, and he was scared.

Doctor Sampson typed into his laptop. "The EKG looks normal. I suspect what you experienced last night was stress related. Your heart sounds fine, and your blood pressure is slightly elevated, but to be safe, I'd like you to schedule an appointment with a cardiologist. I think it's time to run a few tests."

"Okay. I doubt I'll be able to get in to see anyone quickly. Will it keep until after the holiday?" Not that he wanted to wait that long to find out the exact cause of the pain he'd experienced last night, but he was a realist.

Doctor Sampson looked up with a frown. "I don't think waiting would be prudent. I'll have my nurse call a friend of mine. He's one of the best cardiologists in the area, and he owes me one. He may be able to work you in."

Chris's stomach sickened. If his doctor felt it important enough to call in a favor with a friend, then he must be concerned.

Doctor Sampson stood and offered his hand. "Expect a call

from either my office or The Heart Center."

Chris gave his hand a firm shake. "Thanks." He walked out more unnerved than when he'd entered. Now what? He'd begun to plan a future in his head for himself, Rachel, and her son, but now everything had changed.

In a daze, he left Doctor Sampson's office and headed for the ferry. He didn't want to go back. If he ran into Rachel she'd know something was wrong, and he had no answers. He couldn't face her until he knew exactly what was going on with his body.

He'd had a feeling things were about to change when he awoke this morning, so he had packed his suitcase and put all his stuff into his car before heading over to Rachel's. Maybe he should find a hotel on the mainland until he took possession of his house.

Once in his car, he pulled out his cell and phoned the B&B.

"Wildflower Bed-and-Breakfast. Jill speaking."

"Hi, Jill. It's Chris. I decided to check out today rather than next week."

"Is everything okay?" Concern filled her voice.

He should have known leaving the way he did would create questions. He'd gotten to know the staff at the B&B over the past several weeks and had shared his housing plans, but this was too personal. "I have to be on the mainland to deal with something. I sign the papers on my house Friday, so I'll camp out there until my furniture arrives next week. There's no point moving back and forth, and I should probably be onsite when the work crews are there anyway." His argument sounded weak even to him, since he could easily check in at his house and sleep at the B&B, but this way was best.

"Okay. I'll make a note that you've checked out. Your credit card on file will be charged for your stay."

"Okay. Thanks. I hear you'll be at Nick and Zoe's Christmas Eve bash. I'll see you there."

"Great. Take care," she said before disconnecting the call.

He set his phone in the cup holder and sat, unsure of his next move. He signed papers in two days on his house. He wouldn't have any furniture until the following Wednesday, but like he told Jill, he could camp on the floor until then and a motel would do until Friday. A place near the water would be ideal for a couple of nights.

He checked into a rundown looking place a block from the ferry. It wasn't fancy, and it didn't come close to the Wildflower B&B, but it was clean and the bed was comfortable. He could work as easily from here as anyplace else.

He stared out the small window toward the parking lot where the snow had been cleared and wished for his island view instead of the concrete jungle outside.

This was for the best though. He couldn't face Rachel until he knew exactly what was going on with his heart.

He'd been lying to himself. He wanted to live a good long life, not to die young like the other men in his family. Even though he spouted off about being in his golden years, he'd never truly believed he was going to die any time soon until last night. He thought he'd be the exception. He realized Doctor Sampson had told him to reduce stress as a precaution, but his blood work had always come back within acceptable ranges, and his heart had always sounded fine.

His cell phone broke the silence in the room. He answered when he saw it was Doctor Sampson's office.

"Chris, we were able to get you in to see Doctor Zwape at three this afternoon. He had a last minute cancellation and said he'd fit you in."

"Really?" He wrote down the important information and checked his watch. "If I hurry, I'll make it. Thanks!" He grabbed his wallet and keys and darted from the room. Good thing the roads were clear of snow.

Three hours later, Chris walked to his car in a daze—*angina*. How had Doctor Sampson missed this?

The appointment had been brutal. The blood work wasn't

a big deal, but he hadn't anticipated the stress test and echocardiogram. It wasn't a death sentence according to his doctor, but he needed to fill a prescription and also begin taking aspirin to help prevent clotting and make it easier for his blood to flow to his heart. To his relief, the doctor seemed confident this treatment was all that was required at this time, but warned if the cholesterol test came back high he'd add a statin drug to his treatment plan.

He shook his brain free of the fog his diagnosis had caused. This was not a death sentence. His doctor was a specialist and knew what he was doing. His condition could be managed. *Thank You, Lord.*

At least he knew with diet, exercise, and medication he could live a long life, and he didn't have to fear a relationship. He might easily live to be an old man. He stepped a little lighter with the realization. Regret that he'd checked out of the B&B hit him. He'd allowed fear to determine his steps today, and that had been a mistake. He wanted to see Rachel and see if she'd made a commitment to the Lord. He suspected she had, but he needed to know for certain.

He could phone her, but he wanted to see her face when he asked her. Plus that conversation was best conducted in person. No, tonight he'd pick up his meds, an air mattress, and sleeping bag for when he moved into his house, watch some TV, then book a room at the resort in the morning since he didn't care to explain checking out then checking back in. Living like a nomad was growing tiresome, but it was only for another day. After that he'd have the keys to his house.

His cell phone rang, disrupting the quiet of his car. He clicked the button allowing him to talk hands-free. "This is Chris."

"Hey there."

He grinned at the sound of Rachel's voice. "Hi yourself. How did the decorating go?"

"Jason lasted about ten minutes then asked to watch

cartoons."

He chuckled. "I never much enjoyed it myself as a kid, but he'd seemed to want to do it, so I gave him the chance. I'm sorry you ended up decorating alone." He pulled into a parking lot and stopped.

"It's okay. Those ornaments were really neat. Where did they come from?"

"Here and there, but mostly the thrift shop on the island. I added a few clay ones I made as a kid. My mom has given me an ornament every year since I was a baby, so I have plenty to share." To this day his mother continued the tradition. "What are you doing tonight?"

"Nothing exciting. How about you?"

"Same."

"We could do nothing together." Rachel sounded hopeful.

Regret washed over him. "I would like nothing better, but I'm staying on the mainland tonight. I'll be back in the morning."

"Oh." Disappointment clouded her voice.

"How about tomorrow night?"

"I work."

He sighed. Life was back to normal for Rachel while he still tried to figure out normal for himself. "I plan to stay at the resort tomorrow since I take possession of my house on Friday. I feel awkward going back to the B&B after checking out early. Maybe we could get together before or after your shift."

"That might work. Let me talk to Jason's sitter and get back to you. What did you do today?"

"Hold on a second while I disconnect from Bluetooth." He stepped out of his car. "You there?"

"Uh-huh."

He headed into the drug store. "I had a couple of appointments that took forever." A car honked at him as he quickly walked into the crosswalk that led to the store door. Some people were so impatient. "I'm looking forward to getting back to life on the island. I already miss the easy pace." He pulled out a shopping cart and strolled down an aisle, checking out the merchandise. It was good to see more than the basics that the island's general store carried.

Rachel laughed. "I don't know about the easy pace. Jason keeps me busy, but people are very kind. I'm glad to be here." She must have turned away from the phone because her voice muffled, and he couldn't understand her words. "Sorry about that. Jason wanted water."

"How's the little guy tonight?" As he chatted on the phone, Chris easily found the air mattress, air pump, and batteries, but he couldn't locate a sleeping bag anywhere.

"Pretty good, but anxious to get his stitches removed. The poor kid sure has had a time of it since we moved here. Believe it or not, he never had a serious injury or sickness until the last few weeks."

"I still feel bad about his arm."

"You had no way of knowing he'd climb onto the counter. Don't beat yourself up."

"I'll try not to." A bright yellow, radio-controlled car grabbed his attention. Jason would enjoy that. He stuck it into his cart. He walked to the pharmacy window. "May I call you back, Rachel? I have to deal with something."

"Sure. 'Bye."

He picked up his prescription and aspirin and paid for the rest of his purchases. He'd like to get Rachel a little something for Christmas too. Her small house didn't have space for knickknacks. Being a cook, she'd probably enjoy something for her kitchen, but he had no clue what she'd like. He'd spotted a kitchen specialty store on the way here. Then again, he didn't want her to feel obligated to get him something. It was probably best to keep things simple.

He left the store with an extra bounce in his step, and once he settled in his car he reconnected the Bluetooth and called Rachel back. "It's me again."

"Hi. I talked with my sitter. She's fine with coming early. We could meet at one."

"Perfect. I'll meet you in the lobby. See you tomorrow." He disconnected the call and noticed a horse and carriage ahead decked out with Christmas lights. He suddenly knew what he wanted to get her for Christmas and didn't think she'd feel any obligation to him because of it. But he'd have to talk with Zoe to make sure it would work.

CHAPTER SEVENTEEN

RACHEL PULLED HER COAT ON AND kissed Jason on the forehead. "I love you."

"Love you too, Mommy." Her son sat on the couch with a book in his lap.

"Remember to call if you have any questions or problems," she said to her new sitter who'd come highly recommended.

"Don't worry. Jason is going to be fine. I've raised three sons and a daughter, and they all survived." She chuckled. "Although there were days…"

Rachel studied the middle-aged woman. "I know. And Nick said you are great with the kids at church."

Beverly's face tinged pink. "I enjoy children. Now off with you. Don't keep that man waiting."

Rachel grinned and blew a kiss to Jason before jetting out the door. A light coat of snow still covered everything. As beautiful as it was, she wished the sun would either melt it away, or they'd get enough snow to actually have some fun.

She took her time driving to the resort. Although there wasn't a lot of snow, it was a little slick, and she didn't care to end up in a ditch. A short time later, she parked in employee parking and darted inside to escape the cold.

"Hi."

Rachel jumped when Chris stepped from beside a large planter. "I didn't see you there. I thought we were meeting in the lobby."

"I figured you'd come in this way. Would you like to go sit in the lounge or take a walk by the lake?"

Neither. Didn't he realize how cold it was outside? But she really didn't want to go to the lounge either. "Let's take a walk." Good thing she wore her coat, gloves, and knit hat. Otherwise she'd freeze. Even then she would be chilled. This place could use some fun indoor activities for the cold winter months.

Chris grasped her hand, sending tingles up her arm. Maybe taking a walk was a good idea after all. The doorman held the oversized glass door for them as they left. Frigid air blasted her face. She really should buy a scarf.

They strolled along the cleared pathway that led to the lake. "It's so beautiful."

"Much nicer than where I was yesterday. Have you noticed how quiet it is here?"

She nodded. "I think snow softens sounds and puts a hush over everything." Everything except her mind. It moved non-stop. The past few days she'd been trying to learn about her new faith as much as time would allow. She couldn't figure out why her parents had only gone to church on holidays, but she'd be sure to ask them.

She hadn't yet shared with anyone about her decision to follow Jesus and felt an urgency to tell Chris. The path curved to the right and continued around to the other side of the lake.

"You're quiet," he said softly.

"So are you." She bumped her shoulder against his. "I made a decision I wanted to share with you when we came home from the hospital, but you took off so fast."

His face brightened. "Tell me about it."

"After we hung up the other night, I found the chapel at the hospital. I did what you said, and I'm a Christian now."

He stopped and turned to face her. "I'm very happy for you. Do you have any questions?"

"Not yet. I've been reading the Bible a lot and picking Zoe's brain when things don't make sense. She has been more than patient with my questions and even suggested a couple of other books that might help me understand the Bible better."

"Good. I'm happy to clear up any confusion too." He tugged her close and hugged her. "This is the best news I've heard all week."

She leaned back and studied his face. He truly looked happy for her, but his comment made her wonder if he'd had a tough week. "You okay?"

"Better than." He released her and dragged her back in the direction they'd come. "Let's go. It's freezing out here, and we need to move to keep warm."

CHRIS WANTED TO TELL her about his medical condition but hesitated. Everything was perfect between them. What if she'd want nothing to do with him once she found out about his angina? Then again he'd already told her the men in his family all died young, and she hadn't pushed him away. So maybe he was worried for nothing. He glanced at his watch and picked up the pace. He had a sleigh ride scheduled for them in fifteen minutes.

Laughing, she trotted beside him. "You should have warned me you wanted to jog, and I'd have worn my running shoes."

He slowed. "Sorry. I didn't mean to go so fast. Is this better?" He didn't want to spoil his surprise, but they really did need to walk fast. He should have turned them around sooner.

"Yes. Thanks."

"I'm glad we were able to get together today. This next week is going to be packed for me, so I probably won't see you until Christmas Eve."

"That's right. You move into your house next week."

"Actually, I'm moving in tomorrow. My stuff won't be there until the middle of the week, but I hope to be settled by Christmas."

"Good luck with that. Unless you don't own much, I imagine you won't be settled that fast."

"My condo was small and that house is huge by comparison. It will be scantily furnished. But I'll have the necessities." Sleigh bells rang out. Relief surged through him when he saw the driver waiting. "Look, there's the sleigh. Care to go for a ride?"

"Really?" Surprise lit her voice. She checked the clock on her phone. "I'd love to."

He picked up the pace slightly and waved to the driver. Rachel didn't need to know he'd had this planned all along.

The driver stepped out of the sleigh and opened the door. "Good afternoon."

"Hi," Rachel said and climbed in.

Chris sat beside her and draped a thick blanket across their laps. The driver settled on the bench in front and made a sound the horse must have recognized as "go" because he pulled forward.

Rachel slipped an arm through Chris's and snuggled close. "If you don't have plans for Christmas, Jason and I would love to have you come over."

"I'd like that." An uncomfortable feeling gripped his chest. *Not now!* He tried to ignore the feeling but knew he must take his medicine. The doctor warned him against ignoring the pain.

He disengaged his arm from Rachel's and slid the bottle from his coat pocket. He had to pull off a glove to remove the cap then stuck a pill under his tongue.

"Is that what I think it is?" Rachel's brow scrunched.

"That depends on what you're thinking," he teased as he stuffed the bottle back into his pocket and slid his hand back into the warm glove.

"It's for your heart."

"Yes."

"I thought you were okay. That you were only being cautious."

"Me too, but I was wrong. Does this change anything for us?"

She sucked in her bottom lip clearly debating her answer. "How serious is your condition?"

"Angina."

"Is it dangerous?"

He shrugged. "Not serious enough for surgery." *Yet.* "This is all new to me. I found out yesterday."

"Your appointment," she stated.

He nodded and noted the pain had subsided. This was not the way he'd intended for their sleigh ride to go. He'd planned a romantic trek through the woods. "Do you mind if we sit quietly and take in the view?"

She shook her head, but concern filled her eyes.

The driver expertly guided the horse about a quarter way around the lake before veering off into the woods.

Chris draped an arm across the back of the seat and drew Rachel closer. The air cooled as they wove through gigantic firs of some kind. Twigs crackled under the wheels, since there wasn't enough snow on the ground to slide.

"This is spectacular," Rachel whispered and pointed. "A deer."

He grinned when he spotted the four-point buck that the doe followed. The sleigh slowed, presumably so they could take in the view. A hush fell over the forest, the only sound the jingle bells attached to the sleigh. The deer moved on, and they continued forward. At some point they must have woven their way back toward the resort because it came into view as they exited the canopy of trees.

"It's snowing!" Rachel raised her face to the sky. "Isn't it beautiful?"

He reluctantly agreed even though he wasn't a fan of the white stuff, but had to admit in this setting it was pretty special. The sleigh stopped exactly where they'd begun their ride.

Chris got out and offered a hand to Rachel as she stepped down. "What time do you start work?"

"In about thirty minutes. Would you like to grab a hot chocolate?"

"Sure." They strolled to the coffee cart they'd visited the night of the movie, and he ordered them each a hot chocolate then guided her to the same secluded bench. He still awaited her answer about whether his medical condition changed anything, and he was worried she wouldn't answer.

"I have a story to tell you," Rachel said.

"Okay. I like stories." He sipped the warm, chocolaty treat.

"You probably won't like this one, but I think it's one I should share." The unease on her face put him on alert.

"I haven't always been like the person I am today. I was a rebellious teen and didn't get my act together until I found out I was pregnant."

He knew all of this but wouldn't let on he'd overheard her conversation with Zoe.

"When I told Jason, Jasie's dad, that I was pregnant, he said we should get married. It sounded like a good idea to me. Plus it wasn't like anyone else had asked. I didn't love him, and I doubt he loved me, but we were good friends, and I cared about him as a person. What happened between us was stupid and never should have happened, but we were both drunk and..." She shot him a nervous look. "This isn't easy."

He clasped her hand and gave it a gentle squeeze. "You don't have to tell me."

"I want to, so you will understand. Jason and I eloped and

then discovered he had a cancerous brain tumor. He died two weeks later."

"I'm really sorry, Rachel."

"Thanks. But I want you to understand why your medical condition concerns me. I don't want to fall in love with you and have you die a few weeks or months later."

"There are no guarantees in life, Rachel. You could die tomorrow. I could die ten or twenty years from now. We simply can't predict that kind of thing, and I for one have decided to stop stressing about it. Sure I was upset at first, but I decided to live my life the way I want to, and if I die, then I'm going to a great party in heaven. Besides, DNA doesn't determine my future, God does."

Her eyes widened, but he saw a hint of a smile behind the shock.

"Does what my life used to be like bother you? I was a party girl who didn't think twice about what I did. I'm not like that anymore."

"That's obvious. To answer your question, yes it bothers me that you were like that, but not for the reason you may think. I hurt for the young woman that you were. I'm sorry you saw and lived that side of life."

She wiped at her watery eyes.

He grasped her free hand. "You are new in Christ now. Washed clean. All that is past, gone, and you don't have to hang onto the guilt you've been carrying around. This is your new beginning. Some call it a re-birth."

She grinned. "I know. I suppose that's what Christmas is all about. Thank you for not holding my past against me and for not judging me. That means a lot. And as for your heart condition, I like your attitude. You're right that there are no guarantees. Thanks for helping me to see that, but it still makes me nervous."

"Me too, and you're welcome." He grinned.

"I'm so glad I came to this island. Ironically, Jason's the one who sent me here."

"I think I knew that, but remind me how that happened?"

She chuckled. "His parents used to own Wildflower Bed-and-Breakfast. He was raised in that house and lived in the same apartment where Zoe and Nick now live."

"That's right." He nodded. "So you've come full circle."

"I suppose so."

As much as he appreciated her openness about her past, what he really wanted to know was if there was a future for them. Maybe she needed time to process what he'd told her.

"In a way it's because of Jason that we met and that I found my faith in Jesus. It worked out great in the end, but the road here was rocky."

"That's how life is, Rachel. We all have a past, and that past is not always pleasant, but it's what makes us who we are today. I like who you are *today* very much."

Her face tinged pink. "I like who you are too, Chris—angina or not. But don't die anytime soon."

He chuckled. "That's the plan."

"Good, because I like having you around." She drew close and placed a soft kiss on his lips. "I need to get to the kitchen. Enjoy your stay in the lap of luxury."

CHAPTER EIGHTEEN

ON CHRISTMAS EVE, RACHEL AND HER son sat at the B&B dining room table surrounded by her friends. The room was scented by roasting turkey and all the trimmings, exactly like on Thanksgiving, only this meal was more special because it was served in the B&B rather than the little downstairs apartment and there were a lot more people.

Two tall red candles at each end of the long table flickered, and a display of holly and greenery ran down the center. Instrumental Christmas music played softly in the background, and to top off the perfect evening, snow cascaded from the sky. She'd heard someone at work say this year had a record snowfall.

Chris sat beside her. "Are you enjoying yourself?" he whispered.

"Very much. How about you?" How could she not enjoy herself with such exceptional food and good company? Zoe and Nick had outdone themselves.

"Same."

She looked at the faces of the guests at the table—Piper and her husband Chase shared a smile, and Jill and her niece and brother laughed at some joke Nick had told. Rachel missed the punch line and only grinned.

Jason tugged at her arm. "Mommy, I'm finished."

"Okay. Can you sit quietly and wait for the adults to finish?"

"No." He looked at her with big eyes and shook his head. "I need to wiggle."

She held back a laugh, but it didn't stop the rest of the table from erupting into laughter. Her face heated, but Jason soaked up the attention. He sat taller and grinned.

"I think we're all finished," Nick said. "How about we move into the sitting room? I had a piano brought in. It was supposed to be temporary, but I think we're going to keep it." He pushed back from the table and stood.

Relief washed through Rachel. She didn't want a power struggle with her son, and this was the perfect diversion.

Zoe stood. "Leave your plates. We'll clean later."

"Works for me." Chase patted his stomach. "Who's playing the piano, Nick?"

"Me," Jill said. "I've been practicing on the piano at church for weeks, but I'm no virtuoso. So sing loud, everyone."

Rachel chuckled along with the rest of the small group at Jill's explanation. She hadn't gotten to know the B&B manager well, but in what little time they'd spent together, she'd come to like the woman. Rachel especially appreciated how she'd helped out taking care of Jason. Jill was definitely a good addition to Wildflower Bed-and-Breakfast.

Chris rested a hand on her back. "I'm stuffed. I'm not sure I can sing," he said softly for her ears only. "Maybe you and I could go for a stroll down to the water instead."

"What about Jason?"

"He can come, or we can ask Zoe to keep an eye on him."

"Let's do one song first, then we'll sneak out."

He nodded.

She slipped over to Zoe and explained her plan.

A twinkle lit her friend's eyes. "Why not go now? You don't have to sing carols."

"Because I *want* to sing at least one carol."

Jill sat at the lovely baby grand squeezed into a corner of the room and began a rousing rendition of *Jingle Bells*. All their voices blended—well sort of blended, but it was festive nonetheless. Without stopping, Jill transitioned into *Joy to the World*.

Chris laced his fingers with hers and drew her away from the group. "You ready?"

She nodded and looked for Jason. He sat in Nick's arms with a huge smile on his face—he would be fine while they took a walk. She motioned to Zoe that she was leaving and turned from the group.

As much as she was enjoying herself, she treasured any time she could be alone with Chris. She slipped into her coat, gloves, and hat and followed him out the door. A brisk breeze whipped through her hair.

Chris clicked on a strong flashlight and lit the way around to the back of the house to the trail that led down to the pebbled beach. "That was fun."

"Yes. I can't believe Nick got a piano for the sing-along. Especially a baby grand."

"I've discovered that he doesn't do things halfway." Chris moved the flashlight over the snow-covered trail.

"I can't believe tomorrow is Christmas. This holiday season has gone by faster than any I can remember."

"Same here, but I suspect it had to do with your move, new job, passing out your first day on the job, Jason spraining his arm when your incompetent sitter left him alone for two minutes, and then his surgery."

"When you put it like that, this has been a *crazy* holiday season! They say things come in threes, so I think it's safe to say there'll be no more visits to the hospital for Jason and me."

"Good! I'm really getting sick of that place."

Having Chris by her side through it all had helped her face those rough days. Having him with her made her heart kick into double time. She enjoyed his company more than she dreamed possible.

They exited the pathway and stepped onto the beach. A hush came over them as water lapped at the pebbles.

"Look, a shooting star." Chris pointed.

Her gaze darted to the star-filled sky. She caught her breath. "Cool." She closed her eyes and wished for many more times like this with Chris.

"Thanks for coming down here with me." He rested an arm across her shoulders as they faced the water. "It's been such a crazy week with my move that I feel like it's been forever since we had any time together. I've missed you. How have you been?"

"Not too bad. Jason has bounced back from his surgery. He's still sore, but it's kept him calm and made it easier for me to get baking and shopping done. I hadn't gone Christmas shopping at all. Thankfully my new sitter didn't mind a few extra hours the week of Christmas. I went to the mainland and picked up some gifts. Remind me to never wait until the week of Christmas to do my shopping again. It was a madhouse at the toy store."

"Makes you appreciate the slower pace of this island all the more."

"That's for sure." As much as she enjoyed their small talk, she couldn't help and wonder why he'd asked her out here. She turned to face him. "What's going on with you? Are you still planning to come over tomorrow?" She held her breath, anxious for his reply. She'd planned the day with him in mind. If it'd been only her son, she'd have scaled back, but she wanted to make Christmas a special day for the three of them.

"I am."

She let out the breath she'd been holding in a soft whoosh. "Good." A smile stretched across her face.

"Speaking of Christmas, I have a little something for you."

"You do?" She had a gift for him under her tree but hadn't thought to bring it with her. The resort photographer, who she hadn't even noticed, approached her later in the day with the photo he'd snapped of them in the sleigh. She'd had it framed. It wasn't anything big, but to her it was special. She had one framed for herself too.

"I found this at the resort gift shop." He pulled a purple scarf from his pocket and draped it around her neck. "I noticed you didn't have one."

She ran her cheek along the soft yarn. "I love it. Thank you."

"You're welcome." He grasped the ends of the scarf and tugged her close. His warm breath tickled her face. "In spite of everything that's gone wrong this Christmas season, it's been the best ever because I met you." He rested a gloved hand against her cheek. "I think I love you Rachel, and I hope we can spend a lot of time together in the future."

"I'd like that very much." Her heart raced. "And I think I might love you too."

"Maybe we should explore this a bit further." His lips found hers and warmed her from head to toe.

After a few minutes of enjoying his sweet kisses she pulled back. "I could kiss you all night, but we should probably head back. I'm sure Jason is wondering where I went."

He drew her close and held her for several seconds. "If you insist, but I'm going to miss having you in my arms."

She chuckled. "Stop being dramatic. You can hold me any time you'd like." She slid from his arms and moved toward the trail. "Come on, I can't feel my toes anymore."

He clicked on the flashlight. "We can't have that. Let's get you inside." They rushed up the trail and back into the B&B to the final strains of *Silent Night*. Rachel could think of no better way to spend her first Island Christmas than with these people who had all shown her the true meaning of friendship and love.

EPILOGUE

Two years later

ON CHRISTMAS MORNING, RACHEL SAT ON the couch with her newborn daughter tucked safely in her arms while Jason tipped his stocking onto the floor in front of the Christmas tree. She looked at her husband and grinned. "Merry Christmas."

Chris answered her with a kiss. "Would you like me to hold Sophie?"

"Sure." She handed their six-week-old baby to her daddy and marveled at her huge, blue eyes.

"Mommy, Daddy, look!" Jason held up a box set of little cars.

"Cool." Rachel stood and walked behind the tree. "There's something else back here for you, Jason."

Her son hopped up and bolted around to the back of the eight-foot-tall Grand fir. "A bike! I always wanted one."

"How about you take it for a spin after breakfast," Chris said.

"Can we have breakfast now?" Jason wheeled the bike to the entryway of their home. Although she hadn't known it at the time Chris bought the house, he later told her he'd purchased it with her in mind. That was why her opinion of the house had been so important to him.

"I'll have breakfast ready in a jiffy. How do chocolate chip pancakes sound?"

"Yummy!" Jason patted his tummy and jumped up and down. "Can I help?"

"Sure. Go wash your hands."

Chris stood. "I'll put Sophie in her bassinet and be right back to join the fun."

Rachel nodded and slipped an apron over her head. This was their third Christmas together and every year seemed better than the last. They were married in the gazebo at the park adjacent to the hospital the summer after they met. It had been a beautiful July afternoon that she would never forget.

Her parents had come as well as Zoe, Nick, and her friends from the restaurant. Chris's mom and sister had come as well. Everyone had exclaimed over the setting and the beautiful flowers.

She'd worn a strapless, long, white dress she hoped to one day pass on to her daughter. Chris loved kids and wanted more, but she was happy with two for now.

Chris wrapped an arm around her waist startling her from her thoughts. "You looked a million miles away. Is everything okay?"

She rose on tiptoes and placed a soft kiss on his lips. "Better than. I was remembering our wedding."

"Hmm." He tugged her close. "A good day to remember."

Jason squeezed between them. "I want a hug too."

They laughed as Chris hoisted him into his arms. "Better, little dude?"

Jason frowned. "I'm not little anymore, Dad. I have a bike."

"That's right. You're a big boy now. How about we make breakfast so you can show us what you can do?" He set Jason down, and they all got to work. Thirty minutes later, they stood on their driveway in the sunshine. The baby monitor sat on the front porch loud enough to hear Sophie's soft breaths. It hadn't snowed on the island since the Christmas they met, and it'd been a warmer than normal year this year, with no snow in the forecast. She held out hope for January snow, but not much.

Jason straddled his bike with training wheels and took off around the driveway. "I'm doing it," he shouted.

"Way to go." Chris slid his arm around her waist and together they watched Jason. "That's one great kid we have, Mrs. Campbell."

She turned to face him and wrapped her arms around his neck. "We have two great kids. And they have a great dad."

Chris lowered his head and delivered a heart-stopping kiss, taking her breath away.

"Wow!"

He grinned. "There's more where that came from," he said before capturing her lips again.

AUTHOR'S NOTE

I THOROUGHLY ENJOYED WRITING THIS SERIES and hope you enjoyed reading it. Although inspired by Anderson Island in the Puget Sound, Wildflower Island is a figment of my imagination and a place I would love to live.

Readers, thank you for going on this journey with me. I hope you found the third book in the Wildflower B&B Romance Series satisfying.

Kimberly loves connecting with her readers.
You may find her at:
http://kimberlyrjohnson.com/
Facebook https://www.facebook.com/KimberlyRoseJohnson
Twitter at https://twitter.com/kimberlyrosejoh

You may also follow her on Amazon to be notified every time
she has a new book release by using the following link:
http://www.amazon.com/Kimberly-Rose-Johnson/e/
B00K10CR6E/ref=sr_tc_2_0?qid=1433292617&sr=1-2-ent

BOOK DISCUSSION QUESTIONS

1. Rachel was afraid that people in the church would judge her or dislike her if they knew her past. Do you think her fear was justified? Why or why not?

2. Have you ever judged someone in that way, or have you been afraid you might be judged for your past? How did it make you feel?

3. Chris was determined to not have a romantic relationship with a non-Christian. Do you think he was right or wrong and why?

4. Although an adult and on her own, Rachel had yet to create any Christmas traditions. What are some of your traditions and how did they come about?

5. Rachel experienced a lot of trouble after moving to the island. Do you think it was God's way of getting her attention or just the way life is?

6. In the beginning, Chris expressed the desire to have a family, but he was also afraid to pursue that desire due to his family medical history. Do you ever allow fear to prevent you from pursuing your dreams?

BOOKS BY KIMBERLY ROSE JOHNSON

Wildflower B&B Romance Series

Island Refuge

Island Dreams

Island Christmas

Releasing Spring 2016

Island Hope

Standalone

A Valentine for Kayla

Series with Heartsong Presents

The Christmas Promise

A Romance Rekindled

A Holiday Proposal

A Match for Meghan

A Sneak Peek at Book Four

ISLAND HOPE
By Kimberly Rose Johnson

DERRICK TRAINOR SAT IN PIPER GRAYSON'S office. The window view wasn't great considering she owned the place, but who could complain about sunshine and blue sky, even if she could only see the parking lot? His attention shifted to his boss who sat behind her sleek, glass-topped desk wearing a worried look. Unease settled on his shoulders.

"I appreciate all you've done here at the resort, Derrick, but I need to make some changes."

His stomach churned. Was he about to get fired? "I've enjoyed working here. What's changing?"

"As you know, I'm six months pregnant, but what you don't know is that I've been put on bed rest. Effective immediately you will be the acting manager of Wildflower Resort and Spa. I know we talked about you taking over while I am on maternity leave and that you were concerned about the long hours during that time. I hope you can make this work because I'd hate to bring in someone new."

His pulse thrummed in his ear. "No. It's fine. Are you and the baby okay?" He'd begun to make changes at home to accommodate the longer hours he would be working in a few months, but he wasn't there yet. How would his fifteen-year-old daughter Alyssa handle him working sixty-hour weeks?

"My baby and I are okay, but my blood pressure is too high—has been for a while now, actually. I know you will do an exemplary job in my absence."

He nodded. Talk about a switch. A minute ago she looked like she was about to fire him.

"Knock. Knock."

He turned at the sound and spotted a raven-haired woman with pale skin and classical facial features—stunning. She wore a hoodie, ripped jeans, and work boots—not so attractive, but she'd turn heads if she made an effort. Maybe she worked with Chase, Piper's husband, in the gardens.

"Hope." Piper smiled and stood, though a little slower than usual. "I'd like you to meet Derrick Trainor. He'll be acting as manager until I return. You will need to run your schedule by him before you start any work, and he will check over everything done each day."

Hope frowned. "I hope you're kidding."

Derrick shook his head. "I'm sorry, but I'm not following."

Piper waved her fingers in the air. "Close the door and have a seat, Hope."

The woman sat beside him. "Hope Michaels." She offered her hand. Deep purple nail polish covered her neatly trimmed nails.

"It's nice to meet you." He shook her hand then turned to Piper. That unsettled feeling resurfaced.

"Hope is the owner of the electrical company I hired to re-wire the section of the building that caught fire last month. Her company will also be doing all the electrical work for the cabins."

No wonder Piper's health was at risk. She had too much on

her plate. Between dealing with the fire that damaged three suites at the north end of the building, to the construction of the cabins for phase two of the resort, anyone would have high blood pressure.

Hope removed her hoodie revealing arms with several tattoos. He didn't care for body art, but to each his own, or this case her own.

"Derrick, because of your background in electrical work, I thought it would be fitting for you to oversee this aspect of the project." Her attention shifted to Hope. "Having a second set of eyes is no reflection on your quality of work, Hope. But after the fire I'd feel more comfortable if Derrick double-checked everything. Chase will be dealing with the rest of the subcontractors."

Hope's face reddened. Clearly she wasn't happy with Piper's arrangement. He was an electrician by trade but hadn't enjoyed it. After doing odd jobs he fell into his position here as assistant manager. He looked from his boss to Hope. The tension in the room was so thick it'd take a chainsaw to cut through.

"We can talk more later, Hope," Piper said. "Thanks for stopping in."

The woman stood, but to her credit she didn't argue with Piper, though he suspected she had a few choice words for his boss. "Take care of yourself, Piper." She grabbed her hoodie and strode from the room, leaving the door open behind her.

He turned to Piper. "That was awkward."

She wore a mischievous grin. "You've heard the phrase don't judge a book by its cover?"

He nodded.

"It applies to Hope. I consider her a friend, and in spite of what I said, I don't expect there to be any issues."

"Then why am I inspecting her work? You realize an actual inspector will do that?"

She gave him a look that clearly said he was trying her

patience. Time to keep his thoughts to himself. But what exactly was Piper hinting at when she said not to judge a book—or perhaps Hope—by her cover? Sure she looked a little rough around the edges, but if his boss had confidence in her abilities, so did he.

Although he hadn't been in the field for several years, he kept up to date on everything. He didn't want to close the door on what he'd spent so much money learning to do.

"Hunt Enterprises, my father's development company, has used Hope on multiple projects. She does excellent work. I only wish she'd been available to do the job here when we were building. We probably wouldn't have had that electrical fire last month."

This was high praise coming from his boss—but even given her paranoia something didn't add up. Piper was fair and called things how she saw them, whether good or bad, so what was he missing?

Piper continued to talk, and he focused on her words again. "I've arranged for her to stay at Wildflower B&B since we are booked for the summer."

His sister managed the B&B. He almost laughed. Jill was as straight-laced as a person could get. Her eyes had probably bugged out when she saw the art on Hope's arms.

He tabled the thought for now. He had enough to worry about with the new responsibilities given to him today. "Sounds good. I assume you want me to update you on what's going on in the day-to-day operations."

She shook her head. "As much as I want that, my doctor suggested I allow Chase to filter what information I receive."

Whoa. This sounded serious. "Okay." Piper was hands-on. It must be killing her to release control. Besides that, Chase not only took care of the grounds at the resort, he had a flourishing landscape and design business that often had him away from the island.

"Any questions?"

"Not right now. If I come up with any, may I call you?"

She shook her head. "Talk to Chase. He'll stop in every morning and then again in the evenings."

Derrick nodded. Things were about to get very interesting.

HOPE STORMED THROUGH THE lobby and out the automatic sliding glass doors. The nerve! She was highly respected in her industry. Why would Piper want a dude who clearly couldn't cut it as an electrician looking over her shoulder? Piper knew how good she was.

Her phone rang, and she pulled it from her back pocket. "Hope speaking."

"It's Piper. I think I owe you an explanation."

"You don't owe me anything, but if you don't trust me to do the job then why'd you hire me?"

"You and I have been friends since college, and I've known Derrick for three years. He's a good man, but he's lonely. I think the two of you would hit it off."

Hope stopped moving. A car beeped its horn. She waved and moved out of the way. "Come again? Are you seriously trying to set me up?"

"Well…"

"I quit."

"No! Please, Hope. I need you."

"You should have thought of that before you tried to play matchmaker. Does he know what you're up to?"

"No, and don't you tell him either. I can't afford to lose him, not with me going on bed rest. I can't lose you, either."

This was so unlike Piper. It must be all those hormones from being pregnant causing her to behave like a moron. "Fine. But only because you've been a good friend—at least until today. I will do the job and only the job. I will not go out with

Derrick, no matter how cute he is."

"You think he's cute?" Piper's voice rose in pitch.

Hope waved a finger in the air. "Don't. It was only an observation."

"Okay. I'm sorry." Disappointment clouded her voice. "Thank you for sticking with the job. But don't overlook Derrick just because I messed up."

"Whatever." She liked Piper, but the girl was tripping. "I have work to do. Don't worry about anything here. You've assembled a great team, and your resort is in good hands."

"I agree. Don't be a stranger. I'm sure to get sick of myself, and I'll appreciate the company."

Hope grinned and shook her head. She couldn't stay mad at Piper. "I will stop in sometime soon. Catch you later." She pocketed the phone. When she'd arrived on the island yesterday, she sensed it would be a different kind of place to work when the manager of Wildflower B&B looked scandalized by her tattoos; however, she never imagined what Piper had in store.

She headed to her SUV. There was work to be done, and she would not spend the afternoon daydreaming. She grabbed her tools then headed inside to the north section of the resort. The sprinkler system did its job, but the damage was considerable in the affected suites.

On her way through the lobby she spotted Derrick standing behind the counter. He had a Ryan Reynolds thing going on with his dark hair and five o'clock shadow. She'd watched "The Proposal" many times over the years and had always found him attractive. Derrick's broad shoulders filled out his navy sports jacket and looked very nice, but his clean-cut, boy-next-door look wasn't her thing.

Why would Piper think they'd hit it off? They were too different. She was a jeans and T-shirt girl, and he was GQ. Okay, she knew how to dress up and had to in her other life but much preferred her work clothes.

He looked her way and caught her staring. She whirled around and two-timed it toward the wing that needed repairs. Her cheeks burned. That would *not* happen again.

At six o'clock she called it a day, packed up, and headed to the restaurant kitchen. Looking around for the tall blonde woman Piper had described, Hope immediately spotted Zoe, the head chef, and waved.

Zoe grabbed a large brown bag. "You must be Hope. Piper called and gave me your order."

"Yes, thanks." She reached for her wallet.

"Your meals are complimentary for as long as you work here."

"Really? Piper didn't tell me. Well that's a nice way to end a rough day. Thanks!"

"Sure. I heard you're staying at the Wildflower B&B."

"I am. Have you been there?"

Zoe chuckled. "My husband and I own the place. We live in the basement apartment. I'm sure our paths will cross there sooner or later."

"Small island."

"Yep. Have a nice evening. I need to get back to work."

"Okay." With her dinner bag in one hand and her toolbox in the other, she made her way to the parking lot. She spotted Derrick wearing a black leather jacket and chaps, and holding a motorcycle helmet. Well, that added another dimension to Mr. GQ. She walked over to him. "You didn't stop by to check my work."

"Didn't think that was a good idea today." He winked and slipped on the helmet.

"That yours?" She looked skeptically at the Indian Chief Classic.

He straddled the seat. "Yes."

"Nice." She nodded, her curiosity piqued, but she'd never admit it to Piper. "Well, have a good night."

"Maybe I'll see you at the B&B."

"Why's that?"

"My sister's the manager, and my daughter is sort of the in-house sitter for guests. She sent me a text a little bit ago about needing to watch a kid this evening."

"Oh. Okay. Maybe I'll see you." She strode to her SUV struggling to come to terms with this new information. His sister was the uptight manager, and his daughter was old enough to babysit. How could either of those be possible? He didn't look old enough to have a teen, and he rode a motorcycle. She chuckled. His sister for sure didn't approve of that.

Wildflower Island was an interesting place. She was beginning to think she owed Piper a thank you for offering her the job. The people didn't appear as colorful on the surface as her normal crowd, but one didn't have to dig deep to see there was more to the people than met the eye.

Derrick rode past and waved. Her stomach did a little flip-flop. She couldn't go there. He was *not* her type at all, plus he was a dad. She didn't date dads.

Coming Spring 2016

CHRISTMAS SUGAR COOKIES

1 1/3 cups shortening
1 ½ cups granulated Sugar
2 teaspoons almond or vanilla extract
2 eggs
8 teaspoons milk
4 cups all-purpose flour
3 teaspoons baking powder
½ teaspoon salt

Cream shortening, sugar, and almond extract. Add egg and beat until light and fluffy. Stir in milk. Sift together flour, baking powder, and salt; blend into creamed mixture. Divide dough into four balls and wrap in plastic wrap. Chill 1 hour.

On lightly floured surface, roll one dough ball at a time to 1/8-inch thickness. Cut into desired shapes.

Bake on greased cookie sheet at 375 degrees about 6 to 8 minutes. Cool slightly then remove from pan. Cool on wire rack. Makes approximately 4 dozen cookies depending on size of shapes. Frost and add sprinkles if desired.

Made in the USA
Monee, IL
10 October 2022

15607955R00098